For my brother, Stan

ROTTERDAM

DAVID BATTEN

GW 0530774 0

Liquorice Fish
Books

ROTTERDAM

PROLOGUE

To Frisia

On this black night of the North Sea
the cold carbons are more substantial
than our ambitious band, gently rocking
on a retreating whim of ice age,
of interest to wind and current
swaying towards a land we call Frisia,
darkness above, darkness below,
darkness radiating out
from this wooden boat—
ark of our hopes—
human cluster held by the dark,
sailing over routes Neoliths walked
herding their black cattle
tracking the wake of ice,
fearful, we are told, of falling skies,
foundations we sail above
towards a future of motorways,
meetings, motels.

We will arrive thirsty, hungry
to negotiate the next stage
of our migration. Norsemen
Viking voyagers, confident
with a plan
            carried aloft
by the progeny of glaciers
under the aegis of the Arctic.

I

1978: 23 and Tuesday

good to be making money again but dont want to be doing this for the rest of my life the only reason that im enjoying i think i enjoy is because i can see an end to it twenty seven days to go collect cash do not pass go then back over on the ferry to harwich christmas with the folks buy presents ill buy them here and go home on christmas eve yes thatll give me enough time what a shock itll give them me back with money and presents christ its cold colder than i thought itd be early busses never late the wind off the north sea coming all the way from the arctic god itll be icy loading up containers always colder there might only get a couple sit in canteen all day could do with a couple hours kip   ahhh   bout bloody time…

A grey-black Rotterdam morning loomed out of another dawn. Paul stepped onto the bus in a silent file of workers and sat down, grateful for relief from the raw cold, his senses still lying prone and warm. He wondered if he was losing perspective. He left the flat in darkness and returned to it in darkness, put his head on the pillow, closed his eyes, opened them and it was time to get up.

I'm 23 and it is Tuesday. Of this much I am certain. For four years I roamed the fringes of the Mediterranean from Algeciras to Sinai, washing dishes, working in fields and orchards and vineyards—a great adventure. In my narrative I've been driven from home by a constricted mentality that was more interested in 'getting on'—career-building, making money—than growing up, learning, developing. But this woolly language I'm using, to frame a viewpoint, itself seems suspect: too comforting in its woolliness. What happened to the values of the sixties' generation? This question, this loss, increasingly imposes itself on my home thoughts. Although my recollections of the sixties are the simple absorptions of early adolescence, I feel strongly the message from this period—to be judged for my human, social worth not bank balance and that we should live this, not simply acknowledge it as worthy while being resigned to non-compliance. With the progression of the seventies I've become increasingly isolated, out of place, marginalized: was I mainstream? As my friends embarked on careers, knuckled down and began appearing in sharper collars and shoes, I'm still in blue jeans and granddad vests. Yet here I am, obeying a demanding routine, working hard at two jobs to get enough money to go back to what I've escaped from (a sum my friends wouldn't notice inflating their overdrafts) and wearing a long-sleeved granddad vest for its thermal value, not retro cool.

Paul's day had begun. 6.15 a.m. The bus crossed the bridge from the island where his Victorian digs were to the rest of the city. Once over the water he took a tram to Centraal Station, showing his travel pass to an unconcerned driver who indicated with his eyes Paul should move on down the tram. As his stop approached, he braced for the plunge back into the cold air and the short walk through the railway station to a heated carriage.

On the wide concrete steps up to the station entrance, he passed a tableau of Turks and Surinamers, old and young, graven, fixed, awaiting the work ballot. A man in a suit watched the group from a sleek black car parked nearby. An unmarked van arrived, driver silently picking the chosen few with finger point and nod. Tough, swarthy, unwieldy bundles, under bulky layers of clothing, packages of food, drooping moustaches and deliberate, ponderous movements—the lucky ones, off to as yet unknown work. He had recently stood here.

The Universal Worker. Paul's influences had been trade union power plays as portrayed by an increasingly tabloid press: the rise of the worker and decadence (the two somehow combined), overweening trade union ambition, a threat to 'national values'. The trade unions: gestating in the twenties and thirties, breaking the surface of the sixties and dominating the seventies' British political scene. Their spectre of menace and threat helping shape the narrow conservative outlook of the family home, an outlook galvanised by his father, a 'self-made man'. Paul had been sure there were other given truths here, lurking in the shadows of the rhetoric and he felt ignorant in the face of his father's armoury of editorials.

Hands thrust deep into the pockets of his heavy fireman's greatcoat (bought from Scheppen & Schippen with his first Rotterdam wage packet), he marched on through the station towards the platforms. There was no margin for error in his early morning itinerary. He caught a bus to catch a tram to take a train that got him to work just on time. If he paused to buy a paper or drink a coffee, like some casual traveller, he risked being ejected by the mechanism, knocked out of orbit. His most vital possession these days was a travel pass—admission to the network.

Seated in the heated train, Paul relaxed. He looked down at his leaden army surplus boots, self-conscious amid the smart suits and coats, the neat grooming of fellow commuters. He was not embarrassed, just felt out of place. The train pulled smoothly out of the station. He gazed out of the window. The track must have been on an elevated embankment for he looked down through a void onto a shimmering black lake of lights, like stars that define space without illuminating it. Planets of red neon advertised coffee, tobacco, his slow, early morning mind among astral bodies, riding an electric chariot above the firmament looking down through the sky at man's Earth. This *aller-retour* of Paul's day was always dark even though the return leg was quite early in the evening. At least it saved him from having to watch the flat, conquered landscape. Was this route perpetually black? a permanent night corridor from the city to his workplace? or a tunnel to the bowels of the earth where he would load the Devil's cargo to return only into night? He watched his reflection in the window. It looked intensely dramatic and intimate, exaggerated light and shade—not like looking in a mirror but more being close to a near ancestor. He noted the eyes: blue, not bad. His beard, blond and wispy in reality, looked solid here. Yes, he preferred this image to that which he assumed people saw. He looked through the reflection and out into the hollow blackness above the neon stars...

II

Reinhardt

unreal   death   hot   what am i   people looking   cold sweat
shit   cant move   a name what name what   think think what
dont move   dream england was it a dream   where is this
rocking people looking dont move   how did i get where is here
name what name dont move

He did not know where or what he was, knew it would be
explained   needed   time, sit, adjust, allow life to catch up...

This was strange. He had not had a dream he could remember,
had not realised he had been asleep. His body had to remain inert
until a self came tumbling back.

The train had stopped moving. He looked at his hands,
moved his fingers, relaxed to allow a wave of relief crash through
him...

But it was his stop. He leapt to his feet, dashed to a door and
jumped out onto the platform as the train moved off. Cold air
gripped him by the throat, the weather was keener than in the
city. Paul steadied himself, refastened his coat and made for the
exit and the ten-minute walk to the loading yard, emerging from
the station into the unfolding sombre-grey day.

Walking quickly over the cobbled street. Here people
acknowledged him. He was in a small bustling docks complex
on the coast, protected from the onslaught of the sea by
defences of a scale so huge as to emphasise the size of a fear
and fallibility. The power of the sea was indeed feared by the
local people who harboured vivid memories of the devastating
floods of the fifties: living memories of neighbours' floating,

bloated bodies were difficult to dispel. They surely understood, profoundly, the sea was not to be controlled, only held in abeyance.

'Hoi!'

'Hoi!'

Yes, I like it here, the tension: the air, the water, people busy, getting on with transforming matter into energy, the stuff of life. Not being from here, but able to feel a part of it just by being here, helps savour a sense of place, of each day to be relished, a common history shared in the present. Back in Rotterdam folk eventually talk to me of the bombing and Germans and occupation—existence as a memorial, place as history, present existing in past. But out here by the dykes reminds me of arriving in Israel. That was inspiring: people working for the good of the nation, for each other, a communal, social ideal, the kibbutz movement—young and old not haggling or competing over material jealousies but grateful to have a country, a purpose to live and work for. I could have settled there. Looking back at petrified England from that sunny, vital land reinforced the thought. England, old and spent: me, young in a young country. I could have done something there, been of value and been valued. And yes, a tall, blond, hardworking young thoroughbred European seemed to be in demand: the Jewish state offered me instant citizenship...

But he had come to realise this was all wrong. The region was ancient. He began to see the bony hand of feud and bloodletting reaching out of the past and wreaking hideous fury on Jewish-Arab and inter-Arab differences and he could foresee Jew murdering Jew, again. Having made Jewish and Palestinian friends he found it difficult to hold a balanced viewpoint and still retain those friends. This was a level of commitment an upbringing in England's social borderlands had not prepared him for. Here, political discussion automatically discounted the other side's evidence. This was new to him and he had to learn quickly, admit his country's complicity in the turmoil—Balfour and

Lawrence; Palestine bequeathed to Jew and Arab; the forming, supplying and officering of The Jewish Brigade and Arab Legion to fight it out. But these frank acknowledgements didn't gain him standing; in fact marked him as disingenuous, weak. National actions and ambitions should be righteous, history mythologized, legendary acts sanctified, facts sifted and selected. He could see populist logic that led down the path to racial nationalism. It sanctioned murder. Genocide. The lessons not learned from Europe's mistakes—or maybe they had? It appalled him. He would not become part of it.

alone   in the hills of the northern border   night time fire-fight percussive whumps pounding the air lying down in long dry grass not needing sleep eyes wide watching staring up at the stars as salvoes of katyushas and artillery shells correspond   whooshing arcing surprisingly languid labouring across the frontier manmade   shooting stars i could hardly see seeking out destruction   flying overhead between muffled crumpings of distant launches and landings   not afraid want to get close to the fighting exciting luring   real   days pass like weeks weeks like epochs in this cauldron of ambition and revenge   lying here staring up at the stars each detonation stirring the stomach each rocket flying across my mind   start to feel sick sick with the species   rise with the sun   my star still with me   walk to the good fence at metullah to watch the line of palestinians filing up to the gate from lebanon to work in israel to return to shellpocked villages in the evening   watching a biblical people in kaftans and kefiyahs trek up to the checkpoint submit to body searches by young trade hardened recruits   pass through continuing on their way into the holy land with silent dignity walk between two machine-gun towers peering through barbed wired electrified fencing into shimmering lebanon of orchards olive groves green hills valleys   blackened ruined villages remembering a visit to dachau   memorial to european events ovens where white heat turned emaciated humans into ash drawn up chimneys and scattered to the clouds   where i looked through the rusted wire at surrounding living green tried to imagine an inmate looking at that sight   couldnt   yet could imagine arbeit macht frei written above the good fence   a smiling boy   where did he come from   throws an apple over the wire to me   throw a fig in return   staccato megaphoned voice from one of the towers ordering us cease   deadening of wonder   negation of staring up at the stars...

'Hallo Paul!' chimed a resonant German voice, rhyming Paul with 'howl', a sharp slap on the back causing him to breathe out unexpectedly and leave him a bit weak and round-shouldered. Reinhardt seemed to materialise out of nowhere. Paul had once asked him where he lived and received an inaudible reply. The question had been directed more out of conversational politeness than a genuine curiosity and he wished he had been more attentive, because to ask Reinhardt the same question twice was to invite a tedious guessing game.

'Guten morgen, Reinhardt,' said Paul impeccably, with a wry smile. Reinhardt's pronunciation of his name had irritated him at first but he came to decide it sounded less English more European—a de-categorisation.

Reinhardt, the Saxon survivor. He admitted to being thirty-five but could have been fifty-five. Watery eyes set in a craggy, bevelled face, a slack, thin-lipped mouth; his jaw made an unusual horizontal movement when he spoke, grinding words out. Not a tall man, the head looked disproportionately large and heavy, slightly wobbly as if, marionette-like, uncertain of its support, burnt-gold hair, thin and wavy, combed left to right across his scalp and when a strand strayed over his face the pock-marked visage became incredibly expressive, suggesting a tragic, exhausted interior. The first time Paul noticed this it had hit him with an inexplicable sadness and compassion.

'We have much loading today, ja?' said Reinhardt, grinning broadly.

'Ja, if you say so mate.' He knew Reinhardt viewed the prospect of a full day's loading with as much trepidation as he himself. They both hoped daily that only one or two empty container lorries would come through the yard gates; most days there were three or four. It was tiring work and Reinhardt kept up a façade of mocking rivalry and ribbing that Paul found draining and which annoyed him when he found himself being dragged into the same pointless charade—the art of the artless wind-up. But he would not allow himself to write Reinhardt off as simply juvenile or shallow. There were times when the old German showed glimpses of astonishing depth, warmth—the Saxon knight's brittle outer casing, soft human centre—a tenderness and strength Paul recognised and responded to. On balance he knew he liked the man. He also remembered he had once acted less than honourably, which he now regretted.

On the first day, they had arrived at the yard together. Having been sent by the same agency, it was assumed, in that strange, silent conspiracy of competition, that only one of them would be kept on. There was another loader, a large well-muscled Dutch youth, the foreman's favourite. Paul worked with Reinhardt, who constantly paused for a rest, chat and roll-up. The next day, he was paired with the Dutch boy. This was his chance to impress with work rate and quietly express dissatisfaction with his slack competitor, dissent which would hopefully be channelled back to the management. Acutely embarrassed at recalling this act of betrayal, it was with great relief he recalled how the muscle-bound youth's impressive, American-accented English did not match his understanding of the language. No harm done, the folly compounded by the realisation there had never been competition between them; both were needed and hired. Also, a maximum of only four containers per day was possible, no matter how fast they worked. He felt foolish, on moral parole and this helped him tolerate Reinhardt's occasionally infuriating habits and mannerisms. He was in the German's sympathetic debt. He was sure that at some intuitive depth Reinhardt understood this. And Paul didn't mind that it was so.

Perhaps there might not be a lorry waiting for them. They turned the last corner and the yard gates came into sight. They were open, a bad sign. Spirits sank. A container yawned widely, revealing its dark interior. Adjacent pallets, stacked high with ten-kilogram cartons, beckoned. The foreman and the Dutch boy had begun to feed the void, a gesture, of course, to make Paul and Reinhardt feel guilty that they had not been there when the lorry arrived. Though they were not late, the gesture succeeded. No friendly greetings were exchanged this morning as Paul and Reinhardt assumed their positions. Cold as it was they shed the heavy warmth of their coats and took over the loading.

A song was playing in Paul's head from the juke box the night before, in Piet de Bruin's. Every word suddenly seemed relevant to this time and place and the music helped romanticise a few minutes of his life, like the soundtrack to a film in which he sometimes felt himself playing a part. If nothing else it helped him through a glum moment in his day.

Within minutes both were sweating, the sweat cooling icily inside their clothing. Each carton contained a tin of blood-warm, foul-smelling catering oil from a nearby processing plant and was bound by thin nylon straps that soon chafed through the free issue safety gloves. The destination of batches was stamped on the individual cartons: Syria, Iraq, Saudi Arabia. Bad joke, the contrived irony of sending oil to the Middle East. Transferring cartons from pallet to container they soon got into their rhythm and now Paul was actually quite pleased the day had begun with some hard work to warm him up.

Since arriving here from the Mediterranean, coldness has taken on a new significance for me. Beyond the metaphorical, it seems to have acquired a cultural, almost philosophical, dimension. I feel the cold to a depth that transcends physical sensation. During the past four years wandering southern shores I've experienced fast-moving, dynamic relationships, an intensity of living under a hot sun. Here, I have to get used to a more formal, slower pace to relations, as well as the anonymity of living in a large northern industrial-commercial conurbation. The climate, the streets, the quality of life is cold. No sleeping under the stars here. My recently liberated sense of freedom is once again restricted, almost offended. Finding a heated room or sitting near a radiator has come to resemble a spiritual experience, trying to revive something other than cold flesh. Yet the remoteness of this society has its compensations. I need time, a convalescence, a period to adjust, to prepare, gird myself to the prospect of going home. A fading suntan in late November allows me to feel detached enough from my current environment to avoid implied association with it. Yet the real coldness for me, a natural, willing team player, was the prospect of never fitting in, never having a use. The tan will soon go and I will be in England surrounded by countrymen speaking my language. How will I feel about detachment? Personal relationships, remote or intense? How will friends and family see me? Their lives and times have continued for four years, regardless of me, with all the subtle changes that occur: what do I know of England or the English now? These questions concern me because they are gatekeepers to the next stage of my journey. I want—need—to resolve them. Not good enough just to reject—must build a viable alternative I could live for. Believe in. And yet can I? Do I have the faculty, the appropriate machinery? Sometimes, what I face looks awesome, the proportions of the quest seem immense, as if trying to come to terms with the scale of a universe. Am I alone in trying to find a role that fits, that's useful? The only one in the cosmos on such a journey? Am I odd? Going against the crowd—Dad's definition of madness. But it is not depressing. I've decided to grow up in my own way—to explore, work out, discover. Inspiring? Daunting? Mm... kind of irrelevant. The project, starting at year zero—like an Old World explorer sailing into the white space off the map, anticipating the unexpected—is to discover, work out an ethic, an ethical programme that will allow me to look myself in the eye, respect the person in the bathroom mirror, look forward to my day. My contribution to humanity will be to do my honest best, to reach a self-fulfilment—no one knowingly harmed in the process. Sometimes I wonder if those who cold-shouldered me—the disapproving it'll-all-end-in-tears brigade—are not more admiring than they would admit of my evolving life and persistence in choosing a path other than that mapped out for me, and maybe the longer I survive outside of their gravitational pull—where be dragons, true—the more justified, the stronger my project, my alternative, would be felt

19

within their tight, gravity-bound world. Maybe. But the notion, the idea this is a work in progress, balances the doubt involved in the fearsome, exhilarating sensation of wandering lost and lonely among the stars.

By ten o'clock the container was loaded, doors sealed and towed out of the yard. Dripping sweat and red-faced, Paul and Reinhardt dropped to the tarmac leaning back against a wall. The sweat began to cool. It is a strange phenomenon—in icy air yet bare-armed and cold-sweating, somehow unwholesome, unnatural; the skin was hot and flushed, the body not. Realising that another empty container was not waiting outside the gates they donned jumpers and coats and clanged their way up a steel spiral stairway with turret-like slit windows facing out to the industrial skyline, up to the canteen on the top floor of a building that overlooked the yard. As they entered, a wave of steaming air engulfed them. Paul bought two black coffees. The canteen was empty but there was clatter and chatter from the kitchen, the preparations for lunchtime. As he carried the coffees to their table he thought this may be a good opportunity to unravel some of the mystery surrounding the old German. So far he had learned that Reinhardt had been born in Leipzig, had joined the East German merchant navy and whilst his ship was docked on the River Thames had walked into a London police station and claimed asylum. However, this did not explain what he was doing in Holland. Surely a German did not defect from the Soviet Bloc to live in Holland where Germans were still held in almost aggressive contempt. A more pressing question though was where had Reinhardt been last Friday? He had not turned up at the yard for work and Paul was worried he would be sacked. Dutch management tended to have a cavalier attitude towards its foreign non-unionised 'agency' workforce and to miss a day, even for a valid reason, could put you on the 'unreliable' list: one was easily replaced. The foreman had had to work with Paul all day—the Dutch boy preferring to rest his muscles driving the forklift. But yesterday, Monday, on Reinhardt's re-appearance, there had been no dressing-down, no recriminations.

'Well?' He sat opposite Reinhardt.

'Well what, Englishman?' said Reinhardt, sternly, taking the coffee in two hands, the extremes of his crooked mouth curling into a smile over the cup, in anticipation of the game his friend was devising.

'Well, what happened last Friday? Where were you?'

'Ach,' replied Reinhardt, his face now crumpling into a reflection of troubled thought, head bowed looking deep into his coffee cup. 'I go to see my aunty.'

'Ye-e-s,' said Paul, sensing the verge of a discovery, 'and where was that?'

'München,' came the curt reply. Reinhardt stood up and shuffled over to the full-length windows that formed one side of the canteen and stared out.

Paul slumped forward onto the table, resting forehead on arms.

This is a side of the garrulous old campaigner I don't see very often. Curiouser and curiouser. Leave it for the time being. In any case, be wary of finding out too much too soon about those I like. The more you find out about people the less you will admire them—another one of Dad's maxims. Don't believe it of course but keep it in mind. I've lived the last four years in blocks of three months or so, working and moving on. Initially because this was how things turned out, but increasingly as a kind of policy. After about three months some of the shine, the spontaneous goodwill of meeting and working with new people begins to dull and the warts and weaknesses—petty jealousies, self-interests—reveal themselves, which is disheartening. I want to be with, and remember, soul mates, soul community: relationships as remarkable, original, sustaining, beautiful. Know this is possible, have experienced this. But sometimes, sometimes I sense my own openness—which is not an opening social gambit but a play for the long term—being taken advantage of, even seen as some kind of ruse or tactic, which is depressing.

*

However, it was not only Reinhardt's character that drew Paul in. There was an ineluctable sense of tragedy and history about the man he wanted to explore. Was he Europe's war baby? Battered conscience? Germany's refugee alter-ego?

The warrior with the winged helmet pulled his cloak about him and stood motionless on the rock pinnacle that thrust out of the forested slopes. Stars hung around him in the calm before dawn. It was to be a fateful day. He knew what he had to do. Behind him on the western plain were peaceful, prosperous settlements: cow bells occasionally donged, a dog yapped and was silent. Before him, beyond the eastern forest, he imagined hunched, many-limbed shadows stirring, could almost smell the threat of an engulfing wave from the East. He made himself see it. See what he must pre-empt.

Dawn. He squinted into a blinding, blood-rousing sun bringing shadows in which he found the silhouettes of beasts with the torsos and arms of men standing upright on stunted goats' legs and the horned heads of steers. He was sure he could feel the beat of cloven hooves upon the earth through the rock, vibrating the air, threatening. He must act. He drew his special sword and flew down from the heights, protected by his magic cloak and shield, and plunged hacking and hewing into the vile hoard. The battlefield boiled and heaved, bodies bucked and bled, bellowing and screaming. The sun burning gold flashed off the helmet and slashing sword...

we hundred march a mile from camp   army is retreating   no traces to be left behind   starvelings not really alive not really human half-naked clubbed and whipped through the wood to a clearing where the pit has been prepared   these chosen push them in   a moaning mounts and dies down   they disentangle stand upright summoning dignity heads at the height of polished boots   a descending calm   lives departed long ago cannot flash before them   these chosen   the order comes the firing begins the moaning again becoming one voice trying to drown out the harsh clatter   they writhe and knot as bullets tear translucent flesh   at the end of the firing line the character i inhabit has been part of this drama for too long   my trigger finger slackens i am crying   turn towards friends good friends comrades and countrymen and my finger tightens   they twitch dance die stare at me incredulous but know I have struck my own desperate deal stitched myself into the fabric of the fantasy   I turn and empty the magazine into the open-mouthed commander   the man in black falling smoking back down in lush grass   the rifle falls from my hands   survivors crawl out of the pit behind me rising tide of the nearly dead   i cannot face them   feel them clutching at heels coat pulling pulling down tearing ripping   I inhale my own screams...

Looking down on the sinking sun spilling crimson across the sky. Looking down on the aftermath. A tide of blood ebbed and ran west. In the ruddy light, the remains of the settlers lay, smoking or crushed under hooves.

The warrior, drenched in blood and sweat hauled himself up the steep slope towards the rocky pinnacle, the wings of his helmet broken. He paused and looked down on the dark scene he had brought about. What had he done? How had he dreamed this into existence? If only he could get back to the top of the rock, that sacred place, become recharged and drive the scourge back into nightmare. Fortified with new hope he continued heaving himself up to the summit where triumphant horned animal-men were looking down on him... waiting...

The gothic cosmorama began to move from side to side, slowly then violently. Paul could hear his name echoing across a great void. He was being recalled. But he could not leave without knowing the outcome of the epic struggle, hoping the warrior would somehow emerge victorious. He could help fix the story—warn the warrior, reverse the spell—but the calling was insistent and the scene began to tunnel, shuddering away from him...

'Paul, Paul. Wake up Englishman.' He blearily squinted up over his left shoulder, which was being gently shaken, and into

23

the German's aqueous eyes, reflecting... recognition?... understanding?

The substance of the dream was already fleeing the conscious day to play out in its hidden vault.

Paul sat upright, pushed the cold coffee away and closed his eyes as he stifled a yawn.

'What time is it?' he breathed.

'Twelve o'clock.'

'Early lunch then, is it?'

'Ja, what I was thinking.'

Paul flashed a sideways glance at Reinhardt. 'No', he thought.

They went to the counter and slid trays along the chrome bars to the end where they served themselves with ham and pea soup and chunks of bread and returned to their table. Paul broke his bread and floated lumps on the dense soup, then sipped small mouthfuls from his spoon waiting for the bread lumps to sodden. With his head close to the bowl, Reinhardt expertly scooped up the soup with his bread, slurping it into his mouth, holding a redundant spoon in his left hand which also gripped the tilted bowl. 'Peasant?' wondered Paul. Reinhardt was in a pensive mood today, which was how Paul liked him. He felt closer to him the less they spoke.

The canteen was filling up as workers from the processing plant piled in. They were unusually subdued for a gang of workers, the lunchtime release rising more as a low hum than a roistering rattle.

Soup over, Reinhardt rolled himself a cigarette and Paul strolled over to the window wall. The sun was straining to pierce an armour-clad sky. The thought of sun, blue purity and clarity above the cloud, out of sight and out of reach, added to his torpor. He looked down on ant people moving about in the yard, felt a strange god-like responsibility. The truck looked so insignificant, a toy. Reality as a question of perspective, he thought.

Truck?

'Let's go,' Paul shouted. Reinhardt scooped his cigarette

assembly line into a tin and they both ran down the twisting staircase to the cold yard and hungry container.

Not a container as such this time but a Bulgarian trailer that would consume a third more than a normal-sized container. Grimy, flimsy wood and metal affairs, these trailers were to be carefully stacked yet dangerously overloaded, the cargo held in place by a fraying strain of ropes and tarpaulins. There was something cheap, underhand, corrupt about the business.

Paul again suffered the thaw-freeze-thaw process: sudden and extreme with no period for transition, just this oscillating between over-heated rooms or carriages and the chill northern outdoors.

'Do you reckon this one is gun-running, then?' said Paul once they had settled into a comfortable rhythm throwing the cartons into place.

'Oh ja, sure.'

'As soon as it gets behind the Iron Curtain they'll pour out the oil and fill the tins with bullets, grenades, plastic explosive.'

'Ja,' said Reinhardt, picking up a theme, 'and sell them to guerrillas fighting the British.'

'No, Reinhardt, we do not have an empire anymore. We have given it back.'

'Ach,' replied Reinhardt with a guttural laugh, 'so you say, Britischer. And for why this remarkable generosity?' he asked, ferociously rolling his rs.

'Well, it was about time they learned to look after themselves. Besides, we had enough on our plate sorting ourselves out after beating your lot,' he said without reflecting too much on the resonance of his easily-spoken words.

'You talk scheiss, Englishman. You get out before you are kicked out.'

Paul was caught slightly off-balance by the conversation's swift change of direction and sensed he was being led into an ambush of his own setting. He was not comfortable in the role of apologist for the British Empire. Instead of allowing the development of an argument he could not win, he decided to tell the Bobby Moore-Franz Beckenbauer joke about defeats/victories in their countries' respective national sports. Reinhardt looked puzzled.

'War, dumkopf! Your national sport is war!' said Paul, exasperated. Reinhardt's eyes sparkled and Paul realised the old German had caught him out again, his comic thrust deflected and deflated.

'You sly old bugger,' said Paul, grinning.

The trailer loaded, they chatted to the amiable Bulgarian driver as they secured his load. He could not tell them where he was bound for, but did tell them a story of how he had been ambushed by 'bandits' the last time he had driven through Afghanistan, and proudly showed them the bullet holes in the cab door. He had been allowed to continue once the 'bandits' were satisfied he had no electrical equipment in the cab—radio, radar detector, camera, tape recorder. He showed Paul and Reinhardt pictures of his wife and two sons.

They helped him manoeuvre the toppling wagon out of the yard and waved him off on his mysterious voyage. No doubt he could use the luck they wished him.

Paul and Reinhardt looked at each other and said in unison, 'Koffie!' They jogged up the stairs towards the canteen before another container showed up. 'Fancy going all that way without a radio,' Paul thought as they made their way up the twisting stairway.

The steamy air of the canteen welcomed them back. Reinhardt bought the coffees and sat down. Paul was at the window keeping watch. 'Come, Englishman, drink. There will be no more lorry today.'

'Yeah, p'r'aps you're right,' said Paul with a sigh, and sat down.

The canteen was empty: their own domain again. They were exhausted. Paul slumped forward, resting his chin on folded forearms, nose hovering just above the rim of the cup. Reinhardt was sitting bolt upright, tilting his chair slightly backwards. 'There's something on his mind and I'm not going to find out what it is today,' Paul thought, ruefully, thoughts travelling through the window and over the sea to the land of his birth...

Just over there, a short stretch, where I soon will be. A month will pass and all this will be another part of the biography, sediment, the life laid down day by day, stratified, experience on experience to be excavated, to be re-dreamed in the future, to piece together, to make sense of Rotterdam, its meaning, how I had come to be here—where and what it led to—the city's part in my continuing adventure, my work in progress.

Last Christmas at home had been awful. Months anticipating my prodigal return, planning it, talking about it with fellow travellers, excited, raised expectations of having a good time with a loving family, the traditional feast, past differences displaced by mutual love and affection. And then there were friends, my dear, close friends. Not to be. Family wondering what I was there for, what did I want. I couldn't afford presents. Assumed they would understand. Done my utmost to be with them—travelled a great distance, turned down invitations, disappointed others. But once among them, I had to suppress a feeling of resentment comg from them. Surely I was wrong. This was family: *family*. But then, friends also seemed to shift uneasily when I visited, as if I brought some remembrance of a past they had moved on from, did not wish to revisit. Had I become an unwanted memorial? A re-appearance of what and whom they had once been, ought to be, the life they had led, should be leading? Or a reminder of all they didn't want and didn't want for their children? Didn't, don't understand. This Christmas will be different. They will understand me better, be more mellow, realise I just want to be with them, represent nothing but me, have no judgements to make. Yes, this time it will be different. It was going to be a great Christmas and there's Dad laughing leading me into the lounge and here they are family and everyone I've ever liked or loved or admired clapping smiling at me hallelujah what a Christmas present I love you all can't imagine being more happy and I've got all these presents to give away look at this pile of presents I can hardly see you over the great pile of presents in my arms pile of presents all I need now is a cabbage and a Crackerjack pencil why didn't I hear that? words not coming out why did I think that when I wanted to say it must be emotion these presents are warm cartons shit drop them move into happy room greet old friends mouth not synchronised with words with mind voice playing at wrong speed stop being polite tolerating me im alright just give me time to sort out my tongue why are you all smiling dont smile have a problem stop smiling you bastards words coming slowly half-formed perhaps for the best water rushing danger no one noticing imminent danger cant speak should investigate go upstairs legs still work good bathroom door stuck wall of water must grab banister no no theyll be drowned must save thinking slowing down limbs numb must save theyre grey and cold water in room rising dad? you're in colour...

Looking deep into that face he saw decay, disillusion. A blackening. A scream welled up. A great blast of water burst in and whirlpool-churned Paul around the room. On the other side of the swirl he could see his father floating against the direction of the current, seated in his armchair head back, a jagged opening in his neck engulfing the room. Paul realised he was on a collision course. He was helpless to change course or alter his destiny. As he got closer, the room tore open. He fell headfirst. Inside the wound was a cold empty darkness. He glanced back at the room through the crooked, fast-receding hole. Lightning flashed across it.

Thank god I'm out of that... out of that... I'm out...

Paul woke feeling hot, glued-up with sleep. He lifted his head. His forehead felt sticky where it had been resting on his forearm. He became aware he was looking into Reinhardt's close-up face studying his... something... cigarette lighter? Off-balance, slightly vulnerable, as if Reinhardt had the advantage of him.

'You like sleep, Englishman?'

Paul stretched back into his chair, closed his eyes, gathered his senses. This must be like being in a war—short bursts of intense activity, long bouts of boredom and waiting.

'A little work, a little sleep, a little work, a little sleep. I think you have southern blood, ja?'

'I sometimes think so myself, mate,' said Paul sleepily. Reinhardt put his cigarette lighter in his pocket and pushed fresh coffee towards him, the earlier cup long cold.

'You are needing this, I think.'

Paul, yawning, nodded assent and gratitude, slurping at the greasy black liquid as he began to readjust to the external world again.

'Fancy going all that way without a radio,' he heard himself say aloud.

'Ja, very lonely. And dangerous.' Paul loved the way Reinhardt's rich deep voice made a meal of every word, the syllables masticated before being released as something velvety, something delicious and interesting. Like his face, his head— toffee apple made knobbly with clusters of crisped rice, nuts, dipped in chocolate. And how he sometimes pronounced *th* as it usually is in English and sometimes as z or s. He wondered at how Reinhardt had known he had been referring to the Bulgarian driver when he mentioned the radio. No matter, other considerations were catching up with him.

'What time is it?' Paul asked.

Reinhardt feigned difficulty reading his watch. 'Four twenty-three,' he announced with a mischievous grin.

'You bastard,' shouted Paul. His train left at four-thirty.

Paul flew spiralling down the stairway, his unbuttoned coat flapping about him like black wings, Reinhardt clattering in pursuit. The old carthorse. When Paul reached the bottom he looked up at Reinhardt who had stopped at a turning and was gazing out of a slit window. Fading daylight reflected its glow off the gnarled, rutted face. He looked like some magnificent mountain beast perched high up on a cliff face.

'You coming?' Paul called up.

'Ach, no. You go on Englishman. I have business,' Reinhardt replied without looking down.

No time for enquiry. 'Okay. See you tomorrow!' Reinhardt remained staring, silent. Paul ran into the yard and out through the gates, the first section of his day ending.

The freshening air bit his face. It would soon be dark and even colder. He had to lift his knees unnaturally high to avoid tripping on the cobbles as he charged in his clumsy boots towards the station. On-comers, making way for him called out, asking who was invading this time—the Germans again or the Russians at last? Good-natured barracking. He bashfully smiled back. No time to stop.

III

Renana

reinhardt and his sodding sense of humour knew bloody well id be late for work if i missed train ill make it no thanks to what was he thinking through that window why munich what aunty thank god twenty six and a half days to go   renana will now be packing up school books or in camp washing soldiers uniforms shes a soldier   men   soldiers uniforms me i would be showering after sleeping after working in fields since dawn picking grapefruits apples avocados getting ready to eat in refectory   warm   reinhardt behaved himself today more or less have a good talk with him tomorrow he wouldnt let me miss the train would he perhaps he woke me up no   cigarette lighter lightning...

He had lived through exciting, vital days he understood at the time to be momentous. But the contrast between then and now could not have been greater. He existed in a limbo, the body in a window seat on the four-thirty to Rotterdam for the fifteen-minute ride to the city, the mind in a land of olive groves and blue skies, clear warm seas with pristine beaches to sleep on, the world of the dark-eyed Israeli girl he had fallen for.

He had arrived in Israel by mistake. Working at various part-time jobs in the Plaka district of Athens he had accumulated a decent sum of money. Cyprus sounded good, so he bought a boat ticket and set off. The ship docked at Limassol at six a.m. Paul, having set up his encampment on deck, somehow managed to sleep through the docking at that divided island and when he finally woke the ship was approaching Haifa. Israel: closed borders—flying, the only way out.

You like sleep Englishman. Paul smiled through the window at Reinhardt's words. How true, how very true particularly as he was in a state of convalescence—suspended between replaying and understanding the recent past and the prospect of a future's clean sheet. He recalled leaning on the railing of the ferry in Piraeus harbour as it prepared for the voyage. The grey hulls of the ships at anchor merged with the greyness of a sea that reflected a warm, goose-wing grey sky. It was just after the early September rains and floods that heralded the end of the Greek summer. He had looked back past the ships and the harbour up to the encircling mountains that presided over Athens and its port. Protective barrier, or restrictive enclosure? He had been at the annual festival of Diana that night the storms had broken, drinking generous tumblerfuls of retsina under the thunder and lightning. Diana, moon goddess, protectress of youth, bringer of favourable weather to travellers, swift of foot, tall and beautiful, she also brought healing to mortals but was quick to punish with her bow and arrow. (Diana, Roman counterpart to the Greek Artemis, though the organisers presumably felt tourists would be more familiar with Diana.) It had been a pleasant evening but in his memory it became portentous: a good night for examining the entrails of chickens, a night to rattle Roman emperors. He smiled with his reflection in the window: it was getting darker and he was submerging deep into the past…

Standing there in Piraeus I knew I was on the threshold of something. Time in Athens had been mixed—some of it good, some not so. Some people kind, friendly, intelligent. Some sods. City sods. But I expect that. Can live with that. People had different strategies: coping, surviving. On balance it had been a good time: my time. But this is rewinding from the scene I want. History seems to be like that. Wherever I start I need to go back further to understand how the starting point was arrived at in the first place. To have a complete story I have to include everything. Fast forward. Stop. Renana in hospital. Miscarriage or abortion? Kibbutz up in the north, my refuge. I was supposed to be on Cyprus according to my plan. Not even really sure precisely where Israel was. Did know we supported Israel—at least our media seemed to. I knew about kibbutzim from travellers coming the other way. So plan B had been to find one to stay on for a short while to give me time to establish where I was and work out my next moves. Late afternoon, the sun approaching the horizon for a glorious bloody rendezvous, in the kibbutz children's classroom after lessons searching for an atlas but sidetracked by the English language books on the shelves. The children's teacher, Renana, warily approaching this decadent 'volunteer', as the non-Israeli workers were called, on the hunt for young girls, probably. Renana, long black hair, petite, as nervous as determined to seeing me off. She spoke good English and as soon as she established my 'pretext' for being in the room, piled my arms high with every English language publication she could find and bundled me out off the premises. God, she was beautiful…. But this is too far back. Bogged down with detail again. Skip a few months, go on to the scene. But it's so fresh, so tangible. I walked barefoot on the marble floor of the classroom in vest and shorts that early evening, my shadow before me, as the sun set over the Levant. We were to walk back from the refectory holding hands, the warm night air reverberating with the natural busyness of cicadas, perfume of eucalyptus, grateful that our paths through this world had coincided. Mistaking a crossing for a merging. On the verge of being called up for military service but, in love, she said she just wanted to be with me, said she had always hated the thought of war and killing, of blood and revenge and our love was a solid reason to reject something she had been preparing herself to endure simply on the grounds of duty—and peer pressure. I would marry her to exempt her from service, freeing us to plan our lives together. I was in love! Not the first time I had been hit by it but the first time I realised it, as a life-changing force, as an answer: first time as a man. So this was what it was. We did not anticipate the extent or pervasiveness of the powers we were about to confront…

Until details of her evasive action—marriage—were finalised, Renana was compelled to go on induction weekends and long stretches of basic training: a military re-education, with much official theory about who the land belonged to thrown in. It was a difficult period. During one hastily arranged, emotional reunion, she conceived. He did not feel ecstatically happy at impending fatherhood. In fact rather daunted by the prospect. But he did feel that at last they would be able to fight the increasing pressures together—they had shown they were serious—bound by something more than declarations of love. He could see a life forming and stretching into the future. It scared him to think of it but it was a direction. Something heavy, important, serious to commit to—forever. At the furthest point of his journey the rest of his life seemed to lay.

Renana's family were against her marrying an outsider and the state had a stake in her. It would not give her up easily. An abortion would be the ideal solution for all but the young couple. An irresistible pressure on Renana: would it be right to have the child, after all? He had no work, no trade, no money—he was not even her race. And, if they did, could they ever win against weight of family and state? Paul, the outsider, not menaced by existential angst, resisted on their behalf but he alone could not save them.

Did she have an abortion or was it a miscarriage, as she swore on that miserable afternoon in the hospital high up in the Galilean hills? Summoned from his work in the orchard, mind churning, he had hitched, walked and ran up the steep winding road and through the small Palestinian town cowering below the monumental whitewashed hospital.

He was shown into Renana's room. Her bed stood beside an enormous window that reached almost to the ceiling. He looked out on a view southwards of green-mounded Galilee with its steel disc of lake resting between Roman Tiberias and the Golan heights, the pale gold mirage of the Judean Hills beyond that and the opening of the canyon that bore the River Jordan to the Dead Sea, and on, and on. To the west, the Lebanese Hills; east, the dark basalt of the Syrian escarpment. He was looking down Israel's gullet.

He knelt by her bedside. She calmly explained that she had

partly miscarried and been rushed to hospital to complete the process. He listened, determined to be strong, until she finished. He then ceased to be the man, and the boy buried his head in her bedclothes and moaned and sobbed.

Some weeks later, Renana collapsed in a bleeding agony and doctors discovered that parts of the dead child had stubbornly remained in the womb and continued to develop ectopically. Her body survived the assault, but did she? For now she stroked and kissed his hair while he cried himself out. That night he slept alone on the beach.

The train was nearing the city. Bugger! He had not reached the intended scene. Perhaps tomorrow. He looked out into the evening. Neon advertisements again urged him to buy the coffee, the tobacco, the chocolate bearing the formidable names of their merchant patrons, vestiges of Holland's imperial ventures attempting to reflect past glory onto present day products, aligning historic Dutch mercantile power with a drink, cigar, confectionary. All Paul saw out of the window were cold corporate promises and a black emptiness magnified by his failure to recall what he had thought at the time to be unforgettable. He had not forgotten: the essence of the tableau was part of his fabric. He had merely been side-tracked by recalling too many details in the time available in order to savour the experience the more, bring its multi-dimensional truth to the forefront of his consciousness, reconstitute the epic scope in his present: to salvage a piece of the past and live in its memory before embarking on the next act of his day.

No, he had not yet lost any of it.

IV

Unreal City

this is good   isnt it   will i look back and be proud or is this
wasted time   should i be am i building   is this my prime or
wasted time   im pleased i took on the adventure but is what i
have done bankable   what have i done   had a good time   some
of it most of it probably but am i building developing or just
using up time having a good time   hard work this good time
can foundational times be good times   why not   perhaps they
should be as a guarantee   definition of foundational times like
falling in love or proper schooling   ok paul pillar no one of the
ethos ethic creed of your new world   if building the basis of
the rest of your life is not enjoyable hard work its not going to
work   banned forbidden   its what the whole will rely on   a
safeguard   not building a prison thinking it was a fortress
protecting me from fear   fear of   not belonging not being
useful   fear of failing   then fear would be the guiding force
behind me building my fortress prison   that would not be fun
therefore would know that would be wrong   i want   need   to
be independent   independent and free   independence and
freedom are they the same thing   so no fortress then   or
maybe a fortress of me…

Besides, living in seventies Europe, I don't have to pay for
medical treatment, starve or go without shelter. My dad grew up
in thirties' East London, little changed since Dickens, and talked
of it like the world's end, where the world had given up, where
people looked after 'their own'. If Dad's dad didn't work that
week then no money, no food on the table. You relied on 'your
own' for handouts, for survival in the heart of the largest, richest
empire human history had witnessed. The architects of the post-
war era had agreed: no return to pre-war poverty, populist politics

and war—they would redistribute wealth, provide good education, health and equality of opportunity for all. The Welfare State. And they pulled it off, created that platform for us Europeans. I *ought* to be adventurous, curious, ambitious. I *have* to do more with my life than just survive. This is my mission, my responsibility. I owe them.

His vision fazed back from the dark outside to his reflection in the carriage window. He imagined a future self, seeing and judging this reflection that was responsible for that future self's present, for that future self's lived life. Would he look back and be proud?

The train creaked to its halt. Four forty-five, exactly on time. Good. That allowed for the brisk five minute walk to the city centre burger bar and ten minutes to slip on a uniform, grab something to eat and attempt another coffee.

Paul approached the top of the semi-circle of concrete steps leading out of the station. He paused for a moment to survey the open cityscape before him. People continued to flow past, down the steps disappearing in the melee. Filling the space in the foreground was a web of traffic ways facilitating trams, bicycles, busses, pedestrians, cars, interwoven with careful strips of grass and flowerbeds, at this hour resembling black pits. He was looking down at the apex of the city. The scene glittered and gleamed: flashing lights, signals and signs, the ubiquitous neon. From each side of his view tall buildings defined an open, busy space, completing an offset circle half-formed by the steps he was standing on. Where the Luftwaffe's bombs had created gaps like missing teeth in the arc's bite, smooth, modern structures had risen to fill the gaps, now thrusting above their elderly, ornate neighbours. The geometrical space was breached in the middle by a main thoroughfare that led through the arc into the bowels of the city. Another gullet. Paul looked above the maelstrom at the sky. The light of a hidden moon silvered a slender, crooked split in the cloud, dwarfing the city and about to spill out a brilliant, terrifying cosmic truth. The crooked mouth was beckoning to those who would see, singling him out, communicating, connecting.

He stood there, a giant crow on the rim of an amphitheatre, performance over and the crowd filing home. An icy gust furled the coat about him. He buttoned up to the chin—then plunged down. He traversed the central space and passed through the line of buildings opposite, turned off the main thoroughfare into Lijnbaan, a pedestrianised precinct where shops' bright flarings lit up faces. Sleeting rain gleamed off the paving stones. The steamy, sweet tang of castor sugar wafted along the street from a white-clad street vendor's hand painted olliebollen stand, all steam vapour and bright light bulbs like just-struck matches. Men and women wearing shiny leather or padded jackets strode past the shops with that added urgency of last minute shopping or not missing the bus or tram, heading home after work. Not for the first time he felt colourless, out of place, almost transparent as if these people could not see him, as an all-seeing bird flying overhead in the night can only be seen from the ground by an effort. He did not feel less, but was certainly poor by comparison with these well-heeled Rotterdammers.

A short distance along the precinct was the burger bar. He turned down a narrow alleyway and entered by a back door.

V

Night Shift

Paul descended a narrow stairway to the store room below. One side of the room was formed by the steel doors of the enormous vault of a walk-in freezer that sucked the warmth from the room whenever it was opened. Sitting at a table against the opposite wall, the five o'clock shift were having last cigarettes, coffees and snacks before clocking on for the night. Tuesday was not busy. In burger bar terms a nonentity of a day: it made up the numbers, a day to be endured. Only four staff on tonight. And Moroccan Dave. Tall and broad, his bludgeoned features told the story of a tough life. His hair a black halo like magnificent ritual headgear enhanced a fierce aspect out of all proportion to his gentle nature. Not on the official payroll, he ferried supplies up and down the stairs, put the rubbish out and lent a hand in the kitchen when necessary.

There was Yoko, of Indonesian origin, with fine, delicate features and straight black hair. They called her Yoko because these were the only syllables they had caught of her inconveniently multi-syllabic name—inconvenient in the fast, busy environment in which she was now operating.

Wendy was short, African and eternally cheerful, impossible to dislike. Her maternal ancestors had been transported from West Africa to the Caribbean, ending up in the colony of Surinam and put to work on the Dutch West India Company's plantations. Her father was descended from the wave of Japanese personnel imported to supervise the construction of Surinam's infrastructure. Wendy had grown up speaking South American varieties of Japanese, English, Dutch and snatches of her mother's Yoruba. She betrayed no oriental inheritance, only black African and treasured her African links, despite never having visited the motherland. Her happy, uncomplicated nature and simple direct approach made her a popular member of the team. Never considered shallow, she carried instead an air of simple wisdom and maturity that belied her youth.

Mira, tall, straight, thin, hyperactive to the point of neurosis, was the only white native on the working staff, and the only one who didn't really need the job: she was filling in the days before taking up a full-time course in business studies. She had a pinched face and sharp, pointed nose. Constantly chirping, criticising, arguing, her jerky gawkiness disguised an attractiveness that lay in a good-natured depth of generous basic kindness. Her hectoring was usually in defence of another, rarely to protect her own interests. She had a self-deprecating sense of humour which allowed her to enjoy the frequent impersonations of her by the others, aware that she herself was playing a part, a caricature. She was the bane of the managers.

These last were also a disparate trio, ruling over the American franchise, staffed by this cosmopolitan collection of youngsters. They intended to run the place under a tenanted agreement with the New York parent company once they had served their trainee period. Until then they would be under the scrutiny of Company Inspectors ensuring the establishment was being run according to Company Guidelines. On probation. Sami, a Hindu with a soft, pale-olive moon face, large brown eyes and floppy black moustache that crept along the upper lip stretching the ready smile. It was a constant battle for him to reconcile the contradictions of corporate realities and western city life with a Hindu's transcendentalism.

His contrasting colleague was Yani, of Turkish-Arabic descent. Serious, disciplined he strictly applied and enforced the rules drawn up in New York, an inflexibility that had on occasion led to well-liked and hard-working staff being dismissed for slightest infringements. Necessarily unpopular, his mere presence dissolved a lot of their fun. Yet Paul had ambivalent feelings towards him. He had once volunteered to go to Yani's house on an errand and had found him polite and hospitable almost to the point of being ingratiating. His impeccable, smiling wife served snacks—spiced fish—and he had partaken of the Scotch bottle, strictly reserved for visitors only. He had been treated as a guest and friend and it was not good enough to write this off as merely custom or tradition. The spontaneous outpouring of hospitality deserved some reciprocal loyalty and respect. From there on he avoided the wave of dislike that swirled behind Yani's back.

The third manager was Johan, a white Dutchman, though, for reasons unknown to Paul, everyone called him Piet—seemingly a tradition here: patronyms, pseudonyms, nicknames, pen names… masks. Piet and Paul were the same age and Paul felt a connecting, unspoken rapport—a male white middle class-ish bond, perhaps? Piet seemed to have a wry, ironic take on what he was doing (how could anyone take this as a serious profession?), staying on to see how things panned out. A sideways glance, suppressed smile, cryptic answers to the simplest questions—a sixth-form common room approach to the mayhem of running the joint. Still the percentage projections were good for when the three of them would take on the lease.

Moroccan Dave handed Paul black coffee in a white plastic cup. He took a slurp. 'Where's Wendy?' he asked.

'She'll be down in a minute,' said Piet, who usually sat with staff at break times, although there were separate facilities for 'executives'.

'Anyway,' said Piet looking up with a mischievous gleam in his eye directed at Paul 'I thought you lot had abolished slavery. Or is it just that you need mothering, being far from home?'

Mira chipped in. 'It's just a ploy. First she brings you food, then: O Wendy, it would be so nice if you could help me tidy up my flat, I just can't cope. Then: can you tuck me in Wendy, can you read me a goodnight story Wendy, a goodnight kiss Wendy…'

'Alright, alright,' Paul cut in, 'you're only jealous.'

Piet stood up and backed towards the stairs bowing, genuflecting, tugging his forelock saying, 'Yes Baas, very sorry Baas, won't do it again Baas, you count on me Baas…' He backed into Wendy coming down the stairs dislodging the plate covering a bowl she was carrying, spilling a little of the liquid and scalding her wrist. She winced. The plate went spinning over the side of the stairs and smashed on the concrete floor. They stared at the pieces at their feet in a moment of shared silence, which Moroccan Dave broke.

'What you got there little mamma?' His apparent eagerness to offend was usually ignored.

'Sorry, Wendy,' said Piet, concerned he had caused her pain and been caught out acting casually racist. 'Just messing.'

'It's okay, no harm done,' she replied. Piet turned and hurried up the stairs, followed by Yoko and Mira who was prodding Moroccan Dave before her like a bag of ripe washing. Wendy presented the bowl to Paul, a spicy peanut soup. She pulled a brown paper package from a pocket in which were wrapped two chunks of crusty bread.

'Hurry, you've only got a few minutes.' Paul looked up at the clock on the wall. Five to five. The ratchet of time cranked up the detail of his day. Fleetingly, he saw an old man, his face shrivelled, body bent, alone in a bare room next to an oversized hourglass, watching the last few grains of sand run out and trying to remember... anything.

'You needn't... you shouldn't...' he started.

'Shush. Eat up,' said Wendy, rubbing her wrist. And he did. It was delicious. She enjoyed mothering him as he enjoyed being mothered. He was ready for some uncomplicated tender loving care. No over- or under-tones, just a thoughtful friend. He had never managed to consciously 'pick up' a girl. In fact it usually worked the other way round: a girl flattering and picking him up. Having no discernible 'technique' (undoubtedly something to do with having gone to an all-boys school) his own attempts tended towards rejection and humiliation, the realisation of which pleased him to find he couldn't act as a phoney and made him resolve not to waste time and self-esteem in trying. He did see it as a lack, but one he could live with. He had decided that the act of chatting up a girl was a fake, deceitful manoeuvre, the projection of an impressive image, a managed attractive persona that was by definition untrue. He wanted a companion, friend, an equal and let her take the lead as far as timing and depth of relationship was concerned. He had discovered the mystery of sex and understood and enjoyed its ephemeral glories yet wanted to resist its addictive magnetism. He wanted… what did he want? Everlasting glories? Reliable glories? Certainly something more permanent. Want or need? Love? Like a drunk the day after, he too had said never again, knowing he would. Should he try to develop the relationship with Wendy at risk of losing the elements he presently valued so much? To make the first move would change things: for better or worse remained to be seen. He could invite her out for a meal as a way of thanking her for the food she brought him each evening, then play it from there. However he would soon be leaving for England—his cold, waking dream. Was the rational self giving way to a streak of romantic irrationality—would true love conquer all, against the accumulated evidence to date?

'How's your mother' asked Paul, determined to make the most of a rare moment alone together.

'Oh, you know, sometimes up, sometimes down.'

'You're a bloody saint, do you know that? I must show my appreciation for this…' He hesitated.

Wendy intervened. 'How's your friend?'

'Oh, er… she's okay.' Paul went back to the soup, the moment thwarted.

He had told them, the team, that he was sharing a flat but one day had let slip that his flatmate was a 'she' and 'she' was someone he would have to think about later, on the way home.

Two minutes to five. He wiped the bowl clean with the bread.

'That was great. Thanks.'

'I'll go and put the first batch on. Hurry now.' She left him alone.

Yes, hurry hurry hurry bloody hurry, got to be that old man in a hurry. The power those two hands wield over our lives, bits of metal, bits of plastic, numbers—invention of men to control man. Paul took off his coat and jumper, slipping over his head the thin nylon smock-like tunic and put on the regulation paper hat. The notion of adults wearing paper hats, ordained by a corporate bureaucratic body to somehow make them take their identity—representatives of multinational, global ambition—and roles as 'catering operatives' seriously, heightened the unreal party-at-the-end-of-the-world atmosphere. As of a drinkers' camaraderie, a massive inside joke: nudge, nudge. Understood. Life was a game, an unending carnival. There were those who realised and those who did not.

'They'll be moaning about my face soon,' thought Paul. He had had a beard when he first applied for the job and had been told to shave it off; against health regulations, the blurred border between state law and company rules—either way he could be sacked for contravention. Having fine, mousey-blond hair he got away with not shaving every day. But it had grown quite long again. The managers, each sporting fulsome exemplars of moustache, were naturally concerned with enforcing the rules, whether they privately endorsed them or not: rules were rules. So a word in Paul's ear now and again sufficed while allowing him to remain acceptably scruffy.

A minute to five. 'My God, I've got sixty seconds. Oh joy. What to do?' He adjusted his candy striped paper hat, stood to attention, saluted the clock: 'Ladies and gentlemen, my Arthur Askey: I thangyour!' and bowed to the empty room. The minute ticked over. He bounded up the stairs to take his post for the second act.

The day shift was deserting its positions. Wendy had already put the burgers on the hotplate into rows of six by eight. Paul immediately started turning them over with a tool resembling a paint-scraper. He turned on an adjacent hotplate. It would be busy for the first hour. Each hotplate transformed forty-eight burgers from frozen to edible, so at full capacity they were churning out ninety-six in three minutes. The procedure carefully designed and calculated in New York, relayed around the world by training films. The burgers were thin and frozen in columns of twelve. The technique was to take a column and bang it down on its side at an angle to split the burgers like a pack of cards. The meat-based discs were distributed across the surface of the hotplate and were then pressed down under a circular piece of flat metal alloy with a door knob-style handle welded on the upper side. As the last one was pressed the first was ready for turning with the paint scraper and in turn, when the last one was pressed the first one was ready for scraping off and serving. For performing this placing, pressing and scraping Paul was accorded the official job description of 'Chef'. At a table behind him Wendy was laying out ninety-six sesame seed buns with lettuce and slices of dill pickle from plastic bins, topped with squares of a yellow, salty, rubbery substance containing a flavouring approximating cheese.

Moroccan Dave was in charge of logistics, running up the stairs with burgers and buns and tubs of pickles—then down again with empty containers. He kept his eye on stock levels in the kitchen, anticipating demand, not communicating with anyone, smiling, singing and arguing with himself in his own orbit during its collision with this one.

When Paul slid down the last burger onto the last bun Wendy took them through to the sales' point, placed them inside the heated Perspex display unit and returned to prepare another ninety-six buns. Yoko assembled and wrapped the combinations as ordered on the counter and, in spare moments cleared and wiped the tables. The customers moved down the counter with their packages to the cash till where Mira sat at the end of the conveyor belt taking money: the end product. Piet hovered over proceedings, doing a little of everything. The system—clinically designed as it was for mass-cooking, mass-selling to produce massive profit—worked well. The food was certainly filling (judging by the empty packaging overflowing the waste bins outside) and tasty... and yet... it had the aspect of what one would imagine space food to consist. Laboratory food. All the expected tastes were there but the processed, manufactured textures gave clues to the deception—the bread of papier-mache, the meat of jelly-paste and the cheese cleaved to the roof of the mouth and teeth like cooling candle wax. Which, evidently, was what enough people were prepared to pay for.

Six o'clock, the rush was ending. Just one hotplate was operating by seven o'clock, only half in use and not continuously. As production slowed down, other duties were to be performed. The surfaces not in use were to be cleaned, kitchen swept, stores in the room below stairs to be checked and stock cards filled-in. Moroccan Dave had disappeared but would have his uses later on.

As business dropped off, a more relaxed atmosphere entered the workplace. Mira took over wrapping the food and taking the money. Yoko began clearing and cleaning tables and had the opportunity to clean up in the small room upstairs, always a mess where youngsters, outside of adult vision, tended to find other uses for the enterprise's product, mostly involving propulsion. They didn't come here, it seemed, because they were hungry. Wendy replaced Paul at the hotplate, cooking the few burgers and preparing buns as required. Paul took some stock cards and a checklist downstairs to the freezer to assess the situation. Half of the basement room was a forest of freestanding wooden racks for the hanging of hats, coat, scarves, spare uniforms, that had to be passed through to reach the walk-in freezer. The room was lit by a light bulb fixed to the wall opposite the freezer above the staff's break table, so that as he approached the freezer between the racks, pushing past coats, it became darker. He opened the thick, heavy door. This activated a light emitting a weak, dull yellowish glow that sparkled in the white frost on the walls. He closed the door behind him and felt the hairs in his nose stiffen, breathing in delicious, dry frozen air. He enjoyed this. Dim, cold, somehow cosy, somewhere lifted from a fairytale—home of a hobbit or faun: Mr. Tumnus eating sardines on toast in his ice house under the city.

The monolithic procession of the hours marched on. Eight o'clock, break time. A heavy shower had emptied the streets of potential burger victims. Mira stayed on the till to serve the occasional customer: Moroccan Dave kept an eye on the kitchen and the other three took their break together. Food from the display unit was supposed to be thrown away after fifteen minutes—ostensibly to justify the 'fresh every time' slogan, mainly to conform to health regulations—and staff were barred from eating time-expired food directly from the display cabinet. So fifteen minutes before break surplus food would be prepared, carefully wrapped and eventually disposed of in the waste skip outside, to be retrieved by Moroccan Dave climbing into the skip and taking it back indoors to his colleagues downstairs.

Paul tucked into his first 'meal' of the day: a double-cheeseburger and an apple turnover. He didn't feel much like talking. Yoko was her usual self-contained, quiet self and the woman of Wendy was asserting herself over the friend of Wendy in Paul's sensibilities. He was beginning to feel a bit apprehensive in her presence—self-conscious, deliberate. The three months must be up. High up on the wall, next to the clock was a small TV screen which ran training films on a continuous loop, reminding them how to serve customers, prepare food, clean equipment. Someone had thoughtfully muted the sound so at least they no longer had to listen to the monotony of messages in American accents; repeated often enough they achieved their own kind of silence. At first the messages were great fun: they learned the phrases and slogans by heart and subverted them into an absurd private vocabulary. But sheer repetition wore down the fun. Paul remembered, as a boy, repeating the word 'tree' to himself until it became unstable, the letters drifting apart until he wasn't sure what 'tree' meant anymore, until all language started to wobble. Through that exercise he understood the fragility of civilisation.

Paul watched the screen blankly, ate the food as the minute hand silently jerked towards the end of break-time.

Thirteen minutes past eight. Paul had finished two minutes early. 'I'll go and see how Dave is coping,' he said, rising from the table wiping his mouth on a sleeve. Yoko looked up at him over her fried chicken and smiled. Wendy carried on eating.

'Hey man, what's happening?' said a drooling voice. The kitchen was full of smoke suffused with the delicious aroma of a certain team member's weed *du jour*. 'You want a drag, man?' A joint the size of a frankfurter delicately proffered between finger and thumb emerged through the purple haze. Moroccan Dave was slumped in a chair, glazed eyes at the level of the hotplate, feet up on the bun table above his head. On the hotplate a long-forgotten chicken piece blackened and an apple turnover split and leaked into a black, treacly mess. Above, a pall of smoke was spreading darkly across the ceiling. On the other side of the kitchen Moroccan Dave had presumably begun washing up but then found something more appealing to do. The tap left running, the overflowing water had upset a liquid soap container into the sink and was foaming onto and across the floor.

'Mira!' Paul shouted, walking swiftly through to the counter. 'Mira! What the bloody hell's...?' Mira was also slumping, over the cash till, fast asleep. Trade had indeed dropped off. In the kitchen Paul turned off the tap, addressed himself to Moroccan Dave's merely physical presence, accepted what remained of the joint, jerking him to his feet and led him giggling out through the back door, sitting him down between dustbins and returned the joint. He hurried back into the kitchen wading through suds to the sink. He switched on the powerful extractor fans above the hotplates. Wendy and Yoko came up from their break.

'Yoko, clear the tables and sort out the counter—and Mira. Wendy, mop up over by the sink and make a start on the washing up. I'll try to make some impression on these hotplates.' Both recognised the emergency and jumped to their tasks without hesitation; the managers often disappeared when business was slow but could re-materialise at any moment, in which case they would all be in trouble. The noise of the extractor and bustle in the kitchen brought Mira shambling in to see what all the fuss was about. She saw the panic and rushed out to help Yoko. After several high octane minutes the burger bar was functioning normally again, apart from a few drifting wisps of smoke. Sami entered from the shop side. 'Thank god it's not Yani,' they thought as one. Sami twitched his nose, sniffing the air with curiosity as he walked past the till on his way to the kitchen.

Mira waylaid him, not sure of the extent of the recovery operation, grabbing his shoulder, spinning him round to face her. Heron-like she glowered down from her skinny height and fired off improvised sentences. Sami flinched.

'Someone was cooking the burgers while Paul was having his break, some fat caught fire on the gas flame at the back of the hotplate. We didn't know what to do. Who would? Would you? We poured water on it, it made it worse. But it's not our fault. You should have been here. One of you should have been here. The fire regulations here are what? We have never been told. It's illegal. What if there was a real fire? There are no sprinklers, no smoke detectors, just this…' She pulled out a miniature fire extinguisher from under the counter and pointed her razor face at him like a weapon. She was now on a roll, her nervous overacting becoming convincing role play. 'This tiny thing. This is to save our lives? Ja, hullo! I'm the only one who knows it's here. And how does it work? I don't know, do you?' she said, thrusting it at him.

He looked up into her steely heron gaze and without averting his eyes held the extinguisher at arm's length and expertly sprayed Mira from head to foot with white foam for the seconds it took until it coughed and spluttered empty. Everyone stood motionless, silent. Mira slowly prised her eyes open, a brittle white pillar in spatial opposition to the mystery of the shorter, dark other, combined in an embrace of suspended powderised fallout. Moment surreal, as in dreams.

The night bird flew overhead, its instincts and senses alert, accustomed to the growth of the large, brightly lit area spreading over the dark land. Sami's people were sitting beside the softly rippling Ganges, Mother Ganga, praying for continued peace of mind and thanking her for blessing them with enough food for another day and appealing for protection of and good fortune for their own demigods, having flown their world to a western one of adventure, of prosperity.

Thousands of feet above the night bird, a chartered flight was serving champagne where a couple joined the Mile High Club. And somewhere else a child in its mother's arms was slipping into another world for lack of vitamins.

Moroccan Dave, still dazed, loped into the silent tableau. Pointing at Mira he let out a loud belly-laugh, with which everyone joined in. Mira pulled the gentle Hindu to her and hugged him, covering him in foam, thus completing the circuit, rounding off the act in style.

The next hour clicked over. Mira called for Paul.

'What is it?' he enquired on reaching the counter. Mira motioned upwards with her eyes. A commotion was coming from the room upstairs. 'Where's Sami?'

'God knows. What would he be able to do with that lot anyway?'

Point taken. He grabbed a mop and bucket and advanced up the steps. Food fight. Sitting in two opposing groups were about a dozen boys and girls, teenagers, fifteen to seventeen year-olds. Food was plastered across the walls: apple turnovers seemed favourite, milk shakes oozed downwards coating the new contours—Pollockesque in fast food. Cola cups were upturned on the sticky tables and littering the floor. When they noticed Paul standing at the top of the stairs, watching, they hunched forward, arms folded, giving each other furtive looks, stifling giggles: teacher was here, they'd been naughty.

'Why?' Paul asked plaintively, immediately wishing he hadn't.

'Godverdomme! Why?' repeated one of them with his back to Paul and they all burst out laughing. He drew up a chair between the two warring tables and sat down. They were wearing expensive-looking clothes, were clean, white and bored enough to throw food at one other. Paul sat patiently, silently without threat until he became sufficiently present for them to calm down. One of them plucked up the courage to speak in heavily accented but good English.

'What do you suggest we do every night? Go out to bars and get drunk? Go to the cinema? Ja, sorry, there's a limit, you know, to the number of movies you want to see in a week.'

'But when I was your age I had plenty to do,' Paul cut in, too earnestly, 'I played rugby, watched football. We played our records at each others' houses. We talked… music, learned the words printed on album covers, what they meant: love, politics, meaning of life, infinity…' Paul was losing himself. Even to him his words, though well-meant, sounded hollow. He had gone through adolescence in a different era—just a few years between them, yet the gulf was enormous. These kids were having to assimilate adulthood in a moment of the century Paul himself was struggling to come to terms with. As the energy of boisterous behaviour drained from the room he sensed a despair replacing it, displacing him.

'Look,' said the spokesboy, 'our parents grew out of the war with nothing and became successful and rich. They had something to do, to rebuild and build—remake their old world, build a new one. We are expected to continue that, to equal and improve on their achievements. And then more. They think that they have laid foundations for us to build on. They never considered they just may have accomplished the whole thing— and we might not want it: it's theirs. We have not even yet left school and may be as well-off as we are ever going to be. We know two things. First, we don't need pressure from them, and second, that after school there is a big black empty space we are all frightened of falling into.'

Paul was taken by the considered, intellectual force of the argument and felt undermined. He had expected and intended to give some fatherly advice, a lecture, to young headstrong kindred spirits but instead received an eloquent description of how out of touch he was. He was close to—probably in—their black space. He reverted to trying to justify his immediate presence.

'That's fair enough, but someone has to clear this mess up, someone not as fortunate as you, someone who would like to have the amount that's been thrown around for fun in here tonight.' He was going on to say something about poor people but wasn't comfortable with this line either—it would have been something he could hear his mother saying. In fact he wished he could sit with them for longer and perhaps even talk about himself, his situation. What could he glean from his life to date of use to this discussion? He too was negotiating the big empty—could report back from it.

Six black-uniformed policemen wearing body armour, protective helmets and high leather boots, batons drawn, burst up the stairs, followed by the anxious face of Sami. The spokesboy rose to address the leading trooper. A leather-clad fist crashed into his face, destroying his boyish aspect. He sprawled backwards over the table his terrified friends were sitting at. Policemen brutally, efficiently seized the passive youngsters, twisting arms behind backs, lashing out at any hint of resistance, blows expertly aimed at kidneys, knees, the side of necks. Suffer little children. A girl was sobbing aloud, something in Dutch, over and over, tears streaming down her distressed face.

They were frog-marched down to a waiting police van. A policeman hoisted the spokesboy to his feet. Blood streaming from his mouth and nose, he looked older, wise, somehow timeless. Paul, palms gesturing upward, looked urgently into his face trying to communicate he had nothing to do with what had just happened. The boy tried to say something but the policeman was half-strangling him with a baton. He was marched out like a dangerous criminal. Sami sat on a stair, staring, being consoled by Mira.

'Why?' asked Paul for the second time that evening, this time angrily. 'Why send for them? You know what happens.'

'So brutal. So brutal,' Sami was saying, to no one in particular.

'So why then? asked Paul in exasperation. 'I can handle them. They're only kids. I can deal with them. They're not dangerous, not a serious problem.'

'But Paul, I can't. I can't deal with them. They scare me. What will happen when you go? When they get older, bigger, stronger? This is my life, the future all my family depends on. I have bad bad dreams…'

Shaken, close to tears, Sami's pacific nature was not attuned to such situations. He looked up at Paul, sadness in his eyes: here also despair. He, too, looked older.

'Okay, Sami. It's alright. Let's get this lot cleaned up.'

Paul asked Mira what the girl had been repeating.

'She was saying: *But we don't hate anyone.*'

Ten o'clock. A mini-rush of customers had been dealt with but the usual stampede did not look like materialising and Sami gave the order to start the final cleaning, to be closed within the hour. This was a bonus. Normal procedure was to close at midnight and then start cleaning. But tonight had been unusually quiet. The enterprise was designed to operate at full capacity. Empty, at night, it became a garish soulless space—a circus with no acts, no public: a self-mocking irony. Without the distraction of a constant throng coming and going the place was in danger of seeing itself for what it was.

They had time on their hands and thoughts began to turn inwards. Paul recalled lying in a circle around a campfire through the night, the sounds of an invisible sea, each person telling their story, telling of their hopes, fears, plans, passing round a bottle: disputing axioms, testing ideas, uncovering truths—about themselves, their worlds— singing, laughing, crying—bonding— seemed a natural enough way of growing up and relating to peers. Up here in the north he felt cloaked in self-consciousness, constrained.

The evening shift that had started with energy and camaraderie was petering to an introspective finale, each performing allotted tasks, preparing for the opening shift of another day.

Eleven o'clock. Doors locked, lights out in front of shop. Final checks, procedures to be run through, then home. A sudden loud banging on the glass front. Paul walked from the kitchen to see what the commotion was about. Wendy and Mira were mouthing through the window to a gang of drunken, shouting, singing young men that everything was closed down— 'No more food!' The men seemed in a playfully threatening mood, making gestures at the girls, becoming more aggressive as it became apparent they were not going to get access. The fear was having to walk through that lot soon to get home: no busses or trams at this time of night. Paul called up Moroccan Dave— useful at times like these.

Moroccan Dave stood looking out of the full length glass doors, less than a metre away from the rowdy lads, and smiled. Incensed, they, predictably, yelled hackneyed phrases of racial abuse. He slowly undid and dropped his trousers and underpants, continuing to smile at them. The lads were tripped into the studied silence of the unexpected. Moroccan Dave rolled his eyeballs and started pressing his half-naked body, nose and wide-opened mouth against the glass. Then he stood back a little—as they were trying to process what was happening—and urinated up the glass, fixing the foremost of them with wild, excited, bulging eyes. The men staggered back, unable to comprehend this Arabian apparition. Incredulous, suddenly sobered and, in some weird reversal, offended, they hurried off down the street. The staff laughed until they cried: this was seriously funny. Moroccan Dave couldn't see what all the fuss was about, but enjoyed the appreciation, even volunteering to mop up his own piss, happy to prolong his moment.

Paul went down to the storeroom with Sami to assess the stock situation while the others finished off upstairs. The task took longer than expected and time fell away.

'You had better get off,' Sami said eventually, the rest of the staff long gone.

'But if you need me to—'

'Go on, get out of this madhouse, before you are turned into pumpkin,' said Sami, his face gentle and smiling once more.

VI

All From Gaul

god those kids   the cops were kids   once   what happens
what happens to people   what has hasnt happened to me
theyre ahead of me all of them it was like i was their dad   cops
and kids understood each other   the girl the crying girl another
wisdom   she was above them   could see through them   seer
in a violent childish world   foodfights and cartoon cops
chauvinist world of money and order new economy run by cops
and kids   managing their new crises and catastrophes   im such
a novice   thinking a poetry no one will read or hear   the last
four years have been my first day out of the house first day at
school   im still on my first day   all previous life an infancy
her wise tears   christ im such a novice...

Eleven-thirty. Paul had stepped out onto an empty precinct. The
working city shut down at night. The all-night revellers were in
Amsterdam. This city's trade was not invisible and its people
needed their rest to continue forging its existence another day.

Six and a half hours had gone from his life since he had last
considered it. The shops were illuminated caverns: museums of
modern times, arcades of artefacts behind glass. Concrete and
neon were heartless enough with people but without them
became desolate. The city seemed empty behind the fluorescence
and sodium glow, down the alleyways and back streets, on the
waterways that penetrated deeply into this city like open veins
of dark blood; empty and black. Paul shivered and turned up his
collar. The warm afterglow created by the frenetic activity in the
kitchen wore off as he adjusted to the stone-raw night. He came
to the end of the precinct and turned onto Coolsingel, a main
thoroughfare etched with tramlines that led to the bridge he had
crossed seventeen hours earlier connecting his island to the city.

The parallel lines ran before him, an invitation to read between them: passive testimony to recent times—falling bombs, goose-stepping columns, fear and betrayal. This Rotterdam he loved. This Rotterdam spoke to him—had become a home, it began to occur to him.

I like this walk, it gives me time to think constructively, in whole sentences, the day's work done. So, home shall be tonight's chosen subject. Where is it? Is it geographical? If so, that definition's not helpful. Mum and Dad and all immediate relatives born in London, the generation for whom post-war success meant escape from the smog, poverty, crime—and parents. Dad began adult life as an office boy in Fleet Street, graduating to distribution representative of *The Daily Mail*: he thought it a relatively respectable conservative broadsheet—despite its pre-war enthusiasm for fascism—before building up his own mini empire of newsagent shops. New homes at frequent intervals around the country until I was sent to boarding school at eleven. Can someone have always had a roof over their head and yet be homeless, be unsure of where home lies? Disregarding geographical location, home as a concept becomes nebulous yet more consciously tangible   a notion   an agglomeration of criteria, a hairball of ideas concerning what home means to me. The binding feature of this, the adhesive of the hairball, is the warmth   the truth   of the memory of communities of friendship in my life so far. At each of these different times, within each of these communities I have been at home. These homes were transient, ephemeral yet fixed in time: communities of mutual interests, respect and appreciation: and values. I can't go back to the nebulous, can't return to a chosen fixed point in time. Only hope the next community of interests, of friendship—the next fixed point in time—is not too far off. And that there will be one.

Britain? England? Mum's family from Brittany then Cornwall then   Wales. Dad's side   Normans become Cornishmen   a few centuries in Wales. Then the great exodus east or west:

America or London? London it was. So, originally all from Gaul. Perhaps it is geographical. But which bit of geography can I call mine? Peasants worldwide don't have this problem. I'm always saying 'back home', 'when I get home' feels false. England. Right. Right now I would feel more at ease in Jerusalem, would be able to get around better in Athens or   Rotterdam than London or Birmingham or Manchester, would feel more   at home. Yes, in some ways I fear going back, of the uncertainty of   how well they are all doing? No not resentful of their material progress, I feel so good and strong   confident even most of the time   away from them. But when I go 'home' I seem so   feel so   irrelevant, nothing I say holds, there's nothing about me they can weigh or measure, as I speak in their world I fade out of it airbrushed from our shared histories our growings up. Leaving me here alone, orbiting my own planet. Their regard for me seems to move in direct relation to their status as if   if their money plans or marriages failed   their progress structurally altered stopped reversed   they would then be able to reconnect with me   not for advice more for moral support a familiar outside source not contaminated with their progression   for comfort for   for friendship! That's the bloody word. Friendship. And that's all I want from them, the abundance we had before. From here they look pale, cold   strategic   afraid   afraid of me? That I want something from them? That I represent something fearful?   Lost?   That I will turn up on the doorstep penniless demanding payment of the moral debt of personal ties of shared histories?   Or am I a threat? Is there darkness in me they recognise that I can't see   a shadow of the ghost of an existence they have turned away from   alternative to an ideal of progress   success not measured in terms of cars, houses, promotions   If I am an ethic what ethic? What do I do? I seem to have become a cipher of no inherent value in myself but a symbol of   the nightmare of career-neglect, of self-deception by just getting on with things as they arise?   A warning? Children look away this one will come to no good. My way so far has been defined by a rejection of what was mapped out for me. So why this sense of inevitability   of home   the lemming urge to go back? To prove myself in some way they could understand, appreciate, measure? Feels pre-programmed Too rational   a natural order of things.   Like hell.   All this sixteen/seventeen hours a day I'm doing is to buy some kind of security, independence when I get back so I'll be able to find somewhere to stay, I suppose as a gesture   warning   to them so they don't have to fear they'll have to provide for me bail me out pay me off   Don't want them to   Never did   And for myself so I can buy a ticket to somewhere if I ever need to get out   Buy escape   Christmas presents   To buy time to look for a job or study yes if I want. And pride   No, mainly pride. So I don't have to scrounge, be called a scrounger, stay with friends or family because I have no alternative   God! Why go back? It's going to be exactly the fucking same. It's too soon for them to have mellowed. What happened to happenings? Respect for the need to take time off to find inner understanding, peace of mind? Unassailable middle-class youth doctrine a few short years ago. The Vietnam generation won, against the greatest military power on earth in history, took them on with moral weapons and the guns fell silent, the bombs stopped raining down. The Evil Regime swept to oblivion by a peasant army. Another empire down. And now? The flower-power generation cleared the weeds and expected trees and flowers to spring up—we certainly got the vegetables. They should have pulled out the roots, put down poison, dug over the deracinated patch, sowed new seeds, planted new institutions, for new people   our people to prevent the return of the Old Conspiracy, the Old Firm that leads us to a world of fear and blood. The Old Guard became the new gardeners, tended the weeds back, stronger, more resilient. They learned the lessons that we have not. They diversified, became immune, cultivated new peace-and-harmony resistant strains, new hybrids to last, to cope with changing society better than our New Guard—have set out strategically with all their resources to smash the New Guard being diverted, consumed with clearing up the destruction in the wake of the Old Guard's last demise and trying to design a better way forward. They are manipulating our future while we struggle to come to terms with the chaotic present. They are stealing our new world. Robbery by stealth and violence.

Paul allowed his mind to go blank. He always ended up in ever-expanding space when he tried to think things through, leading to a black hole of thought, sucking him into a pervasive feeling of helplessness, a numbing sense that the best one could do was tend one's own patch and hope for the best. Exactly what he thought he was resisting from those back home. He knew this would lead to blinkered selfishness, greed. A community of competition was what he had left behind in England, home. A logical conclusion he feared was that their mode of life was inevitable and he would end up in it; the difference being that they had intuitively started off where Paul would arrive later by not finding an alternative. Nevertheless, rationalising his life in these terms gave him something to lean on—made him feel more justified in undertaking the journey he was on, a handrail shaky, but solid enough to give him some balance on his uncertain path. He yearned to meet his contemporaries, his family outside of their context, equally naked. He always seemed to bare his soul to them on their home ground, in full armour. All their hang-ups were probably just side-effects of the process of adjustment to new situations—job, house, family. If only he could meet them, unarmoured, equally naked, equally honest, away from their businesses, mortgages, double-garages, school fees, ballet classes, squash clubs: they would probably be terrified.

Nearby, someone was about to die. The screech of tyres echoed softly around the empty streets and mingled with Paul's thoughts. Silence. Then a dull thud and the powdery tinkle of glass smashing and scattering into silence again.

VII

Magda

The upper ironwork of a bridge loomed out of the murky distance. The Maasbrug, site of desperate fighting between Dutch marines and German paratroopers holed up in the National Insurance Building on the northern tip of the island in 1940. He had left the brightly lit commercial district behind. The city was darker here: the street lamps' orange-brown, colour-stealing rays the only illumination in the thick damp air. The bridge was a huge girder construction with three lanes for both directions of passage and pedestrian pathways suspended below either side of each carriageway. As Paul approached, flashing red lights and a lowered barrier warned the bridge was raised. A major event during the day causing queues of traffic and drawing spectators. Tonight, he was the lone observer. A strange sight, a chunk of motorway opening up to the sky, broken white lines leading up into the darkness, up to the stars. The cloud cover had cleared and, away from the city centre lights, the sky was bejewelled. He leaned on a railing waiting for the ceremony to finish. An enormous freighter, unlit, sinister, bristling with cranes like monstrous insect antennae, slipped silently past him: a vast silhouette, dark shape passing through darkness, blotting out buildings, deleting whole sections of the island on the other side of the bridge, towering over him. He felt his own presence shrink. There was some kind of undermining, dimensional shift taking place, like childhood deliriums of waking in the familiar room where the walls and ceiling start to fly away. Close your eyes again to make the room come back to you. But here you are, floating in the eye-shut dark. Open them again to find the walls and ceiling further away, reaching out to touch the wall beside your bed to bring it back and finding the hand itself stretching further and further away.

*

The ship vanished, the road whirred back into place, barrier lifted and the red lights turned themselves off. Paul walked to the centre of the bridge and leaned over the rail, staring out into the black ship-shaped space that had swallowed a whole other world of iron and steel. Ripples against the banks, cosmic sensors, the only indicators that something had been here. Things on this non-human scale carried with them their own reality, their own laws, as if there should be a traceable hole in the air, a portal. He tried to understand that minutes ago a profound mass had passed through where he was now standing watching the river artery heal over. Yes, this Rotterdam he loved.

He was nearly home and had not yet addressed the problem of Magda. Paul had been staying in a flat with the brother of a Dutch girl he had met in Israel. She had given him the address, as travellers do, if ever he passed that way. Paul had left Israel at the beginning of September and flown to Paris with the intention of grape picking in the southwest of France to earn the money to go home. Having slept all the way, he stepped off the midnight flight from Tel-Aviv—tanned, sun-bleached hair, wearing a vest, shorts, sandals—into a grey, drizzling north European September amongst the umbrella-ed, sharp-heeled and be-suited. Rebirth into a stark reality after a stroll in the sunny hinterland of his dreamworld. He hitch-hiked down to Bordeaux, then Toulouse in search of work but found that due to a wet summer the season had been delayed and the wine-producing areas were saturated with people seeking any kind of work to fill in the time before picking began. He had worked in this area before and knew that the majority of pickers were poor migratory workers from Portugal or Spain whose needs were greater than his. He didn't want to hang around on the off chance of landing a filler job at the expense of one of these workers. So, he decided to head for the Dutch address. At least he would have a roof under which to shelter from this northern weather as winter approached.

Life with the brother, Willem, was… interesting. Mid-twenties, tall and chubby he had a long oblong head with short, cropped hair, bulging forehead, thin-rimmed spectacles, goatee beard, rounded cheeks and a red cupid's bow mouth. His sister had told Paul he was crazy, which Paul took to mean a bit wacky, alternative. Willem was indeed alternative. He dressed in a suit every morning and left the flat carrying a briefcase in one hand and brown paper bag in the other. Paul never discovered the contents of either or where he spent the day. Willem boasted of attacking women at night (declared himself 'hurt' when Paul smiled as at a misfired joke: 'Why won't you believe me?'), frequently insisted on petty trials of strength such as arm-wrestling (the one time Paul accepted the challenge Willem lost), had an obsession with American pop singer Blondie (her image plastered around the apartment) and professed to be studying, in his spare time, to become a doctor of medicine. Willem had designs on Magda, a trainee nurse and his sister's close friend who lived in the flat above.

Magda was tall, slim with curly, shoulder-length raven-black hair, clear, pale skin. She laughed a lot when with Paul, but was it the brave laughter of a vulnerable single woman from the top floor flat in the dark building above the Faustian-gothic, unfathomable figure of Willem?

Paul only lasted a few days with his quixotic flatmate. Magda soon came down to talk. He had already accompanied her to a social event, an invitation accepted innocently enough, not fully realising he was perhaps being used, not unreasonably, by Magda to fend off Willem, which in turn would explain Willem's hitherto inexplicable alternating remoteness and increasing aggression towards Paul. After the coffee had perked and been poured she confided that she had always been a bit wary of Willem, particularly since his sister had left. She was sure Willem sometimes followed her when she walked to and from her work at the hospital late at night. Paul suggested he could move up and share her flat—in the circumstances this might be the sensible thing to do. Magda's obvious delight at the suggestion lighting up her face concluded the matter. He never saw Willem again and the friendship with Magda blossomed. He found work and everything seemed fine until it dawned on him that she was falling in love with him. He allowed the relationship to develop. He liked Magda, enjoyed her company and presumed he would eventually fall in love with her. It was a matter of time.

The relationship did, of course, progress, but clumsily and in uncertain direction. He graduated from sleeping in his sleeping bag on the sitting room floor to Magda's bed although she made it clear to him she was not ready for sex. Intimacy, yes. This initially confused Paul—emerging from his recent, emotionally supercharged world, not sure whether to take this as a rejection or sign of serious intent—but he came to be quite thankful with the increasing awareness that in his present state he found he could not love her. Which saddened him, but could not deny it to himself no matter how much he wanted to love her. He had been living a sham for the last month. He faked a bad back ('all that lifting', 'ought to lie on a rigid surface') to get out of Magda's bed and slept most nights on the floor again. He found it increasingly hard to meet her eyes. He wanted to avoid romantic entanglements but needed her friendship. And he really did value her. She was his closest friend at this moment. It was too easy to reason that he would soon be leaving and this chapter closed. And yet that was the most likely outcome. Would he reply to her first one or two letters and then let her become a sad piece of the story he would always carry around? If only he could resolve the relationship without lying, without hurting. How? The more he thought of his predicament the more he realised how much Renana had meant to him. Not that he had ever doubted the extent of his feeling but it seemed to be exerting itself, forcefully. She had become part of him. His mind split in two: every thought had been processed with her at the forefront, every plan, every idea, every dream. She had been the first person he had willingly totally committed himself to. Perhaps his emotions were putting up defences against once more being put through the disorientation he had suffered when he and Renana were being pulled apart. Perhaps he would never be able to love unthinkingly again. Perhaps his inner self would never again tolerate total commitment to another, too cynical, too aware of the fickle qualities of love. Perhaps he had become old. Did no one have the need or ability or confidence to give themselves totally to one giving totally to them? Did no one remain the same? Constant? He had not yet learned that remaining the same involved change. He was a good team player. He hoped his base values were honesty and loyalty; these being repaid with manipulation and strategy had caused him pain and, worse, disillusion. He wanted to believe in everlasting love. He would rather be walked on—and realise it—than knowingly misuse someone else: one of his moral pillars. Was he misusing Magda, though? He feared the ethic of the era he was fast approaching was going to be 'the walked-on are losers—the walkers-on shall inherit the earth'. Where could he go to have his own sanity-preserving qualities appreciated? Not home, where the ethic was already taking root.

In Willem's flat Paul had discovered Dvorak's 9th Symphony, *From the New World*. The piece had captured his imagination. It filled his head as he continued looking out into the darkness, half expecting the freighter to re-emerge like an unbidden truth. He felt the music in all its wonder and trepidation, its optimism, its tragic premonition. Daunting, thrilling.

I know I'm on the edge, the verge   of something. I feel strong, excited, frightened, stimulated, vulnerable, powerful. What is out there, beckoning? I see a future: no money changes hands, just a show of identity, everyone has continuous credit. People have large stomachs, thin limbs and translucent skin, eye sockets red-rimmed, hair thin and wispy. They look pale, cancerous and sick. Outside of their sealed housing units they wear breathing apparatus. Children are all deemed at risk, are forbidden to speak to adults other than uniformed officials of the state—not even to their parents—and have to live in special secure centres. Women, old and young are not allowed on the streets after lighting-up. Colours are bright, toxically bright like toadstools or deadly coral. Everyone has a car, eats fully and dresses well: no one is too cold or too hot or hungry or homeless or redundant. But tension, latent, is in the air. The threat of spontaneous violence lurks wherever people gather. The police force is a body-armoured, masked, feared force trained in crowd control to preserve the status quo and the protection of property. People are locked up—or disappeared—without recourse to justice or a mention on the news. Everyone's wealthy, life cheap. Birds migrating from blackened lands fall from choking skies into brown, dead seas   I can make another world exciting and healthy with human values   of co-operation and trust   free from guilt and drudgery and fear   not easy to see it but can almost breathe it. The land is green, the oceans blue. The air smells of brine and pine, the ruins of mechanisation lay neglected and overgrown greened   my lot have won   they've dismantled the Old Order: long live the New Order—no, too fascist—long live the *Original Order*, the human order, a regime serving all, ruling for the benefit of the populous, us, not in spite of us, not for the control of us...

I know, of course, my lot have lost. My 'hard' future is based on what seems to be happening and its complete vision comes unbidden, like the ghost freighter. My ideal is a conscious, willed construct. And yet, I've had an insight into what an alternative could feel like—communal living in my communities of interest, my 'homes'—the power of combining, organising with friends and fellow travellers at school, on kibbutzim, winegrowing co-operatives, living under canvass, cultural exploration and sharing—a sense of togetherness, in-it-togetherness. This is sustaining—could be sustainable—worth working at and worth living for. And it does work: it is powerful. It gives me hope, a liberation of thought, has vanquished demons, released pressures that built when caught up questing for the grail of 'security'. I sacrificed self-respect and peace of mind, unknowingly, to take my place in the queue, to take my fill of the ever-filling cup of consumer capital. Despite the unhappiness, it had been surprisingly easy: everyone was doing it, everyone I knew. The family encouraged it, society facilitated it. I didn't have to get on with people to earn, to succeed—I didn't have to like them nor they me. Didn't even have to like myself. There was no real friendship—as I knew existed—involved. Just rapport, mutual back-rubbing. In fact the system seemed to thrive in the absence of close ties—it's not personal, just business. Make money, play the game and you gained a certain respect. And 'security'. Only my unhappiness challenged the system. If there was one thing that sustains me, it's my instinctive, natural rejection of that rationale. I could manage the part that didn't require me to like or be liked, could just about cope with the necessary loneliness. Was prepared for personal sacrifice. And I was good at making money: the system liked people like me. But I had to like myself. I need to wake up in the morning looking forward to my day, face myself in that bathroom mirror. I now realise I've always had a working concept of how short and futile a life really is, worked out life was not worth sacrificing for an ideal or principle or system unless the process of sacrifice was itself enjoyable, nourishing, sustaining. If a person truly enjoyed working in a factory or office or bank or shop, then do it. But don't do it and be depressed for the whole of a life for fear the alternative may be worse…

Making the break had been difficult, really difficult even for one as unhappy as he had been. He was not a 'grown-up': he still had an adolescent mindset where ideals are difficult to override, where good and bad still matter. But once the break had been made, life took a spiritual upturn, seemed more real, like finding the key to a mystery. Things became clearer, simpler, logical. Even the tough, lonely parts he could now relish. He liked the shifting, unpredictable nature of this new life living off his wits, personality, ingenuity. His mistakes were his mistakes—he could do something about them, at least own them. His relationships would be his discoveries. One of the toughest times, a December night in a small tent by the Dead Sea, washing strung from the guy rope of a tent pole to a scrubby bush that swayed the tent in the dry, strengthening wind—an initiation in utter loneliness became, through the telescope of retrospect, a spiritual, foundational experience as he lay on the sleeping bag, candles on the rucksack beside him his altar, his Ark of a few personal, treasured minerals—a piece of coral from the Red Sea, a glass tumbler from the festival of Diana, stones from Jerusalem requested by an exiled Palestinian friend, a phial of coloured sands from Sinai. Propped up on an elbow reading enlightening, profound works or scribbling random impulses in a notebook, made sacred by candlelight: imagining what the next day would hold, or where he would be in a month's time, his absorbing ritual, his dream exercise. Precious moments. Here he felt more secure than he had ever felt when surrounded by gleaming goods in a well-appointed flat, regular salary, money in the bank, paying policy premiums, ticking off the years to when he could cash it in. Where he went next was worryingly uncertain but he felt confident enough that wherever he ended up, whatever he did, if he was unhappy he would now have the ability, confidence and courage to find a way out. Self-development, self-improvement were going to be his guiding principles. Ambition, outside of these parameters, was already an alien notion. As far as he could see ambition cultivated greed, lust, power. Sod that. He wasn't going to get caught up on that treadmill. No. He was to be his concern, his responsibility. Happiness the priority.

Intoxicated with the churn of life, he crossed the bridge and onto the island of Noordereiland as Dvorak played out a final flourish.

VIII

At Piet de Bruin's

loving friend   for that is what you are   in the cold clockless hours of the town   the town asleep the dark tired town   the resting wharves   stilled cranes   moored barges   where I am walking towards you   you waiting for me in the cold clockless hours   speaking to you as I will not when I reach you   you loving in love believing in me as I do not   seeing something in me worth loving that I cannot   step by step closer to the truth of not speaking to you as I am now speaking to you   as I should speak to you   should say *tonight the bridge was raised where red lights flashed alarmingly   warning me not to go further into that viscous dark a shape out of the night becoming huge and towering   gliding by on the river   the way forward lowering into place   beckoning me into in that silent space*   imagining you helping me decipher this living dream loving friend   in the cold clockless hours I try to imagine you and me…

Paul walked the half mile along the main road from the bridge to the other side of the island where another giant iron mechanical engineering feat carried the highway off the island and on across the city to link up with Europe's matrix of routes, its life-blood's mesh of veins. The dark little island was a stepping-stone, its larger existence unseen, passed over, as the stream of expensive people in gleaming cars—the red cells of the system—flowed on its way to the brilliant cities.

He turned off at a right angle, south onto Prins Hendrikkade before the second bridge and walked along the unlit waterfront, slowly, letting his mind settle. He had not resolved anything but at least felt reassured he wasn't neglecting or avoiding thinking about difficult issues in his life.

*

A few Rhine barges were tied up and now abandoned by their German captains for the comforts of the shore. Germany had not yet been forgiven by the city for the bombing of its heart in 1940. In the time he'd been living on the island, Paul had tapped into what he discerned as a deeper, darker sense of guilt and complicity that scarred the nation's psyche, its anguish of the soul. He had read that Dutch volunteers were among the largest national groupings in the Waffen SS. Collaborators high up in the present establishment seemed to be exposed in the press with embarrassing frequency. He had heard stories of shady blockade-busting operations of the earlier war: read about a German-related monarchy and the comfortable exile granted to the Kaiser; been told about the shameful abandonment of the Jews; the abject apology of the church for its co-operation with the occupiers. And further back, the still half-uncovered horrors of slave-trading, of Dutch colonial violence in the East Indies—somehow this guilt too seemed to feed into a current of reaction against all things German.

However, much of Noordereiland had been spared the murderous bombing that had crushed the city centre. Here one could read hand-written signs declaring 'Hier Spricht Man Deutsch'. The complexes of the city passed over the life here. Germans were working people, people who needed food and drink and a bed and companionship. Germans had money. Wasn't making money the driving force of the city? Paul liked the island for its air of live and let live. No place for paranoid ideological pretensions. He loved its deep, narrow dimly-lit drinking dens embedded in the ground floors of the five or six storey Victorian façades, felt at home among the prostitutes and bargemen—and Germans. Just sitting, observing, listening, There was less tension here. In the dark recesses you became eyes, a voice—a spirit. Discretion and privacy were important values here: a dark dreamworld hinterland forming for him, here in the cold north.

He turned into the bar Piet de Bruin. It was like entering a tunnel, walking inside the length of a barge: a dark corridor. Where the space opened out, the only light was a red neon tube illuminating the bottles and optics on the shelves at the back of the bar. It hadn't taken long to become a regular and he was greeted with a smile by the tall, heavily made-up barmaid. Without words she poured *twee pilsjes*. He took the small glasses of beer and walked to their usual table where Magda was already sitting, having also bought two beers.

'Hoi.'

'Hoi.' Paul sat next to her. She hugged his arm and watched his profile closely as he guzzled a beer down in one, her shining eyes reflecting a fleck of red neon.

'How was your day?' she asked deliberately, adjusting to speaking English, and smiling.

'Oh, you know—loaded lorries, cooked burgers, Sami sprayed Mira with fire foam, Dave got his knob out and pissed at customers wanting to come in to eat. You know, usual.'

Magda chuckled, not completely sure she'd heard right, and pressed for details.

Having satisfied the need for some idle chatter about their respective days he stood up to put some music on the jukebox. A dull sepia glow lit the song titles as the coins slotted into place. He pressed the buttons for their favourites which, at a tastefully low volume, materialised around them. These were the songs of the summer, of the realisation that a life with Renana was not going to be and yet a stubborn refusal to believe this could be so. The music brought it back to him, conjured the smell of her skin, her breath; he remembered her strong black hair on the pillow, her large brown eyes close to his, heard her giggle, her voice with tears in it. He was no longer in Rotterdam. He was tracing the contours of her nose, lips, chin, tasting her kiss, feeling the warmth of her body, seeing the candlelight sparkle in the tears on her cheeks, remembering the times he had hurt her by his immaturity—that hurt now.

He stifled a sigh. Despite having talked it through with himself and understanding the inexorability of it all, he could not rid himself of a guilty feeling that there was something he had not done but could have: a letter, a number he had known, missing from the equation he could have supplied. All the love, the plans staking out the future they had once eagerly talked over. His old stump of original brain hadn't registered she was no longer with him, that he no longer had a claim on that future. What was it, what was the missing factor? He remembered his mistakes but these were the calibrations of any relationship. Surely one was not punished so cruelly for such when so much goodwill, so much love... when hate and anger were absent? Why the guilt, the self-blame? Why so much trust in goodness: where the triumph of love?

He felt old tears welling up as he listened to the words of the song about watching birds migrating south for the winter while it being forever autumn in the minstrel's heart now his love was no longer with him. His eyes glistening, he wondered what Magda must be thinking. He had, of course told her about Renana, as you would a good friend. She was staring into her glass, listening to the music, suffering her own pain in silence as the next record lowered to the turntable.

Paul drained a second glass. He brushed a tear from his face, peering through the fug at the drinkers at the bar as through a two-way mirror. Saloon-bar women and large-framed men silhouetted against red neon exchanged bar stools and partners, bought each other drinks and bought each other and left. At nearby tables voices of the unseen talked quietly, anonymously. He was insignificant.

Paul and Magda sat silently listening as the records played, allowing him time to recover. He reached for her hand and squeezed it before standing up and leading her from the bar.

IX

Corridors of Light

The cold night tasted of coal. Magda huddled close to him in her big scarf, mittens, fur coat and woolly tights. Paul drew her tightly to him. They walked slowly along the silent waterfront, Paul looking at the stars above the blackness of the island, feeling relaxed, drained. This silent, physical communication was comforting.

Magda unlocked the front door and he followed her up the narrow stairs. Unlit by night or day, spiralling upwards, a dark corridor from one existence to another.

The sitting room was already warming; Magda had left the paraffin heater burning. Paul went straight into the shower as Magda changed into a nightie and flower print satin dressing gown.

Icy, scalding: he stood suffering the oscillations until the dribbling shower reached its compromise. Eyes closed: soap, rub, rinse, dried, done. He wrapped a towel round him and moved smartly into the bedroom. Old, holey tracksuit bottoms from schooldays, woollen rugby socks, T-shirt and the thick knitted jumper Magda had bought him.

She was kneeling in the main room setting out a backgammon board by the soft orange light of a table lamp, pretty in her gown. She looked up at him over her shoulder, smiling, her black curls tumbling. Record playing, percolator bubbling, thick yellow advocaat to sweeten the strong coffee, and brandy: this place, this moment. This home.

They sat on the floor in front of the fire playing the game, drinking the coffee, the brandy: laughed and talked and talked. He felt wide-awake. From day's start he had been so tired, drifting in and out of a sleepy consciousness during every lull.

At this other extreme of his day he felt he could go on and on. This was his kind of time, what he was after and wanted to prolong, put in the rucksack with the other artefacts of his ark. But the moment he dreaded approached: his dishonest moment.

One-thirty, time for bed. Paul tidied the room. Magda went into the bathroom. As the cast-iron taps gurgled and splashed he braced himself for the bedroom act: his nightly death.

At last, Magda stepped out of the bathroom.

'My back's still playing up,' Paul mumbled. 'Be best if I sleep on the floor again. Won't wake you up in the morning then, either.'

'Okay. See you tomorrow night', said Magda, voice guarded, neutral. She climbed into her bed, watching as Paul bent down to gather sleeping bag and underwear for the morning from his rucksack. He pretended not to notice her, lost in rummaging through the bag.

'Heel! Fucking heel,' he silently blasted himself as he carried the bundle from the room, as if it would make any difference, as if the act of self-chastisement could in part exonerate the lie.

He made a vision of saying goodbye, could see them parting, affectionately, passionately even, embracing through layers of clothing on the December-snow frosted platform as the train waited to rush him to the ferry—what was the hurry?—just hours away from home. The train pulled out. He looked back, her hand raised in farewell. Freeze-frame; love's arrested development. His fault. A love that didn't fit, both knowing they would never meet again. The train gathered speed. Rotterdam, an ending.

Paul laid out the sleeping bag on the floorboards, set the alarm and turned the heater down to its lowest. He made a pillow out of his morning clothes and took off the tracksuit and jumper. He poured some brandy into a mug and set it down by his encampment, turned out the light and slid into the bedding. It was suddenly soundless. Alone again. Leaning on an elbow he sipped the brandy. The ruddy glow from the heater's mantle lit the air around him but not the walls or ceiling: he was suspended in a red glow, timeless again. He lay down, hands behind his head... beer, coffee and advocaat, brandy... warming... closer to himself, feeling better... corridors of light... a remembered character by Palestinian shores   casting off the day's grip remembering the character encountered by an Arabian shoreline gently rocking now in a narrow wooden bed

as a hand of wind nudged our flimsy vessel through an ancient sea   a golden sea   through corridors of light   voyaging back with a crew of three a foreign friend her and me   on a timeless sea to a landscape hewn from a dream from before the journey   now floating on gilt   voyaging back to pink rock and a thick sea below earth I can see in its entirety from pink cliffs   a canyon of thought from childish dreams never cast off landscape in my mind that echoes back to the beginning of failure crisis tragedy   floating over the canyon imprinted with massacre and suicide   with scavengers that silently turn and wheel above the plateau's ruins watching   watching waiting for a return to the canyon floor   ravens in the ruins watching   they had been there they had seen   picked it clean the silent bony canyon the skeletons of settlements   echoes of suffering on the wind blowing through the empty dry canyon beautiful   troubling   it was here the answer was here skeletons of settlements and one on the plateau   we stand here die here   shadows filing through empty streets   filing through corridors of light   ghosts ghosts of love and lives and nations   black eyes cast no light into caves where vanished families left their scrolls   shadows cast on stone   shadows that move when I am not looking   the desolate fabric of tragedy still playing out   echoing along the canyon and through my sifting spirit   depositing knowledge guilt complicity in the decadent truth   there an empty bullet-riddled worm-eaten settlement forsaken   even bones sun-salt bleached forsaken   the pillar of the salt canyon turned its back on the suffering   Thou Shalt Die   an oasis a mirage of sweet gurgling green on the right and more salt   brittle mushrooming up from the ground at the end of the thick dead sea I would walk on   hurling itself up at my flying spirit being drawn in which plays no blood-natural part in the ancient earthly drama still running in the parched valley denuded by fiery breath…

the tortured spirits reach out for me   call to me this black night trying to tell me   why me?   tourist   voyeur   as a storm howls down the canyon in a black rage dancing around my tent picking at my tent troubling my sleep   see me turning and turning from the howling of lost skulls coming down from the black cliffs as the dead sea boils and rages around the fulcrum the tent of me   while the skeletons of unspeakable times dance the grotesque step outside plotting to pull up my home and hurl it spinning into the burning black foam…

    voyaging on past the troubling moment of no connection into the calm next day but the sky knew   I read the sky now the souls quieten and darkness retreats up into the cliffs and the skulls become the quiet cliffs which mask the high desert of bones so white it burns into my eyes

on down the throat of rocks and thorn and fire purging flowing on ethereal currents tasting no salt feeling no fire and out into the waiting widening clear deep blue

stretching out into clear space voyaging on

becoming clearer

X

Carry On

lying in snow

      warm in my coat thick black coat

looking up at white frosted trees

        against white sky

beauty of white

    feeling warm cosy that crow is watching me

crow in a tree of crystals the tree

        a whole snowflake

a forest of black branched snowflakes arrested

      in silence perfect white silence

warm lying here in my coat

          cosy
the crow in the tree of crystals

       is watching me
white branched tree against black sky's

         star
black branched trees against white sky

        of suns
I'm flying with the trees

  lying in warm snow flying the gleaming universe

far off machinegun pecking at the mind's forest

The alarm woke him. Didn't remember sleeping, felt heavy and tired. Had to dress quickly, keep hold of the last of sleep's warmth. He crawled from the sleeping bag, pulled on jeans and jumper and turned on the percolator to re-heat the coffee. The heater's paraffin had run out during the night and the chilled room smelled of cold gas. He went into the bathroom, brushed teeth, slooshed face with icy water. Back into the room, turned on the table lamp, sat staring into space as he sipped the tepid coffee, hands trying to tease some warmth from the mug. Any other time, the bitter liquid would have been undrinkable. But the cold taste was something else he would always remember. Were these Golden Days? Surely.

He laced up work boots, hauled the coat over his shoulders. He walked silently into the bedroom. The orange glow from the table lamp reached Magda's sleeping face. Spirits sank when he saw her tear-crusted eyes. He gently kissed her lips and tiptoed from the room with no glory, no credit.

The door creaked shut behind him and he was away down the unlit, ice-cold staircase. He reached out a hand into the darkness towards where the door should be, lifted the invisible latch and plunged into a perfect, twinkling-black new day.

EPILOGUE

Netherland

My ducts of brackish water not coming
      or going, patient, waiting it out

distillations of the centuries' depressions
      gathered in the gloom of Old Master skies

and cried down on my delta of Europe's
      outpourings—my acquiescence.

Even mad Vincent had to escape
      my darkenings, my disembodyings

my potato-eating lands but never
      eluded the stalking insanities

my assassins.
      In late afternoon the crescent moon falls

towards a spire on my splayed horizon
      while progress builds an Atlantis of me

an offering, waiting the sea's promise
      and the sea its signal from the moon